Fox Hunt

Fox Hunt

FOX HUNT is available in multiple formats including

E-Book: 978-1-944336-63-9

Print: 978-1-944336-64-6

Fox Hunt

THE STALLIONS OF THE HIDDEN E RANCH

If two is better than one and three is better than two, then seven must be better than just about anything.

I was on the run from my past when I met Liam—the man I thought was my one true mate. But when he took me home to his ranch, I found out he wasn't alone. Seven stallion shifters own the Hidden E Ranch, each ready to make me theirs, with Liam leading the charge.

Horse shifters mate as a herd, something we fox shifters know nothing about. But I'm ready to learn, and my seven stallion mates seem more than happy to teach me.

———

For the latest release information, additional content, and promotions, sign up for Ellis Leigh's newsletter.

For new release announcements only, follow Ellis on Bookbub.

Chapter One

No one had ever said life would be easy, but if mine got any harder, I was going to have to throw in the proverbial towel. Too bad I couldn't afford to buy one.

"That'll be two dollars, ma'am."

Ouch. I gave the gas station clerk a pained smile and dug into my change purse, counting coins and hoping for the best. Almost gone—I'd spent nearly every penny I'd taken with me when I'd been forced to run from my home. A tragic event for sure, but I only needed to make it through one last leg of my crazy journey. I had enough for the Push-Up Pop in my hand. Just barely. Definitely a win in my book.

"Here you go," I said, handing over a sad collection of dimes, nickels, and pennies—not even a quarter in sight—before smiling brightly at the man behind the counter. "You have a nice day now."

He grunted, his gaze dropping from my eyes to my full breasts and staying there. Typical, though the fact that my dress was about a size too small certainly didn't help matters. I'd have said I should cut back on the sweets, but I knew that wouldn't be happening. Sugary treats were the only thing keeping me going at that point.

I spun away from the counter, the short skirt of my dress flaring and my dark hair flying, before hiking my backpack onto my shoulder and heading outside. The sun blazed down on the parking lot, blinding me and practically melting the cheap plastic of my shoes. Locals could talk all they wanted about this dry heat business—dry or not, a hundred-plus on the thermometer was too hot. Perfect weather for ice cream, though. I dropped my sunglasses over my eyes and tore off the paper to my cold treat as I sought a shady spot to relax.

A few more hours, and I'd be at my final destination. Just one more leg on my trip across the country, and I'd be holed up at the fox shifter sanctuary with the rest of the runaways and rejects. One more bus ride, to be exact. Nice thing about buses—they didn't require you to use a credit card or show identification to buy a ticket. Which was good, because if I'd left any way to track me, if I'd somehow gotten messy and left behind of a shred of evidence that would indicate where I was headed, I'd be dead before I got there.

My inner fox peeked out from where she hid inside my mind, sniffing, interested in the treat I held, but cautious. Always so cautious. The fallout I'd been through over the last few months had shaken her all the way down to her core. She'd gone from a typical fox—ballsy, sneaky, and confident enough to be brazen at times—to a scared little ball of fur. But her sweet tooth hadn't lessened a bit, which was why I didn't mind spending my last two dollars on something as ridiculous as a Push-Up Pop. She needed it, and we were almost to our new home. Almost safe again.

At least, I hoped we were.

I was right in the middle of the first lick of my citrusy treat when I felt a familiar sensation—eyes on me. Someone watching. A shiver of fear shot up my spine as I looked up, terrified of what I'd see. But instead of the short, light-haired man who'd been the worst mistake I'd ever made, there stood a different man. One who was tall and dark and as hot as the sun itself. He might still have been a mistake—most men were—but for just a second, I didn't care.

His long legs were encased in dark jeans, a short-sleeved plaid shirt pulling tight across his chest and arms, and a hat—a real, honest-to-goodness cowboy hat—sat perched upon his head. I'd never seen someone so gorgeous in real life, never been around someone with such a muscled body. And his stare—so deep and intense. Directed right at me. Even my scared little fox noticed the weight of it, the intensity.

And we both liked the attention.

I held eye contact as I took another lick, thinking about all the ways I'd like to use my tongue on him. All the ways I'd like for him to lick me instead. Something made me want to give myself to him right there in the gas station parking lot. Something that also made my heart pound a little faster and my pussy grow a little wetter.

He warned you not to even look at another man, let alone drool over one.

I shoved that thought aside as the man walked closer. No words from my ex mattered at that point. All that did was the dark-haired, blue-eyed man before me. The one watching me with something close to hunger on his strong face. He looked like some sort of model for a calendar, like a cowboy ready to lasso himself a lady and take her home to his ranch to dirty her up a little. I liked that thought. A lot.

Too much.

"Good afternoon," my handsome stranger said, his voice sliding over my body like warm honey. He tipped his hat—actually *tipped his hat* as if we were in some sort of old movie—and gave me a smile that I felt all the way down to my toes.

Trouble. I was in so much trouble.

"Hi. Do I know you?" I took another lick of my ice cream, his eyes following the movement of my tongue. I wanted to do it again, to tease him, to wrap my lips around the treat and see if I could make that heated stare burn hotter. What the hell was this? Never before in my life had I felt such an attraction to a man. This was almost…too strong to resist. Almost. Sort of like what other shifters had described as a mating pull, but incomplete somehow. Not all-consuming but close. Completely confusing for sure.

The man before me didn't seem confused at all, though. He looked me up and down, pausing on my full hips, stopping for a good long look at my breasts before giving me another one of those killer smiles. "No, ma'am. I'd definitely remember meeting you."

Smooth. Very smooth. "Oh. I thought, since you were staring at me and all, that maybe we'd met and I'd somehow forgotten."

Not that I could have. No woman would forget meeting a man as handsome as this one. One with sex in his eyes and a fire burning behind that charming smile. Deadly. The man was deadly to things like resolve, modesty, purity...and panties.

His smile grew all languid and steady, like a slow sunrise on a cloudy day. All that delicious warmth directed right at me. "I was staring because you're the most beautiful woman I've ever seen, and I wanted to make sure you weren't just a figment of my imagination or some sort of mirage. Would have been a shame to see such a vision standing here and have her disappear before I could tell her exactly how lovely I thought she was."

I fought the swoon. I fought it as hard as I could. "Ah, so you're a sweet talker?"

"Guilty as charged." He stepped closer, breathing me in. Surrounding me in his addictive scent—sunshine, warmth, and a little bit of lemon. The deeper whisper of a shifter tickled my nose, but not that of a fox. Not a wolf either. Something different, earthy. Something intriguing. "I'm also completely honest. How'd someone as pretty as you escape my notice in this small of a town?"

"I'm not from here. Just passing through, really."

His eyes darkened for a moment, taking me by surprise. That expression made him appear almost dangerous, but in the best way possible. "Aw now, don't tell me you're leaving so soon. I haven't even gotten a chance to learn your name yet."

"I'm Waverley." *Wrong name. Wrong. Name.*

A twinge of fear raced through me at my slip. I should have lied to him as I'd been doing all along my trip, but for some reason, I couldn't. Couldn't think of the name I'd made up when I'd thrown my stuff into the backpack on my shoulder and run away from my life. Couldn't come up with anything but the honest truth. I sucked at being incognito, at least around handsome strangers in cowboy hats.

"Liam." He held out his hand. Rough, callused, and thick, his fingers wrapped around mine and held on, so much bigger than my own. So much stronger. The sparks shooting between us ignited something deeper, stoking a fire in my gut and making my fox chatter in my head. My breath caught. I stared into Liam's eyes, unable to look away. Drowning in the sea-blue color. Suddenly wanting to feel how soft the black hair peeking out from under his hat would be. Needing to know what the muscles cording their way up his forearm tasted like.

Wet. I had become ridiculously fucking wet from just a handshake. What was *wrong* with me?

But our moment ended too quickly, interrupted when the bus I'd bought a ticket for pulled up. Brakes squealing and engine roaring, the rolling trash can of a vehicle loomed over us in a way that instilled fear within me. That sent a sense of panic skittering across my mind. If there was one thing I'd learned from my recent fall from safe and comfortable into terrified and in danger, it was to trust my instincts.

My instincts told me not to get on that bus, but how could I not?

"That's my ride." I sounded defeated—heartbroken, really—even to my own ears.

Liam glared at the vehicle over my shoulder, looking ready to fight it at any moment. A funny thought, though I couldn't bear to laugh. I needed to get on that bus. Doing so had suddenly become the last thing I wanted to do, but I had no other options. No choice in—

"Don't go." Liam's words exploded out of him, his grip on my hand tightening.

If only. "But I'm supposed to be somewhere."

"Stay for a day or two, then. You can take the next bus that comes through town."

My cheeks burned, and my words tasted burned and bitter as I said, "I really can't. I spent my last few dollars. If I miss my bus, I won't be able to afford another ticket."

"No problem. I'll buy you a new ticket right now so you can leave on the next bus."

So confident, this one. So intense. Hard to resist for sure, though I had to try. "This is crazy. I don't know you, and besides—I'm supposed to be in Fairview tonight. I have a job waiting for me there."

"What kind of job?"

"Cooking. I'm a chef, and the place is a ranch of some sort."

"You don't know what kind of ranch you're heading for?"

I shrugged. "I'll be spending all my time in a kitchen. Whether they raise horses or cattle didn't really matter to me when the opportunity came up. It could be a llama farm for all I know." Foxes and llamas—I almost laughed at the image of that mix running around on some far-off field.

Liam grinned, looking quite a bit like the cat who caught the canary. "Funny thing. I happen to own a horse farm up the road called the Hidden E, and I could use a cook. No bus ride to Fairview necessary."

That was...awfully convenient. "Are you offering me a job?"

"I'm offering you whatever you want. Just come stay with me. I'll buy you a ticket to Fairview right now for the next bus out of town in case you hate it. Though, you won't."

Cocksure, this one. And he was offering me whatever I wanted? I *wanted* to stop running, to have the comfort of a few extra dollars in my pocket again, to know that when I lay my head down to sleep, I had a good shot at waking up in the morning instead of worrying someone would break in and kill me in the middle of the night.

I wanted normal.

Liam and my attraction to him seemed anything but normal. And yet...

"You're not an ax murderer, are you?"

He laughed so loud and brash, it dragged a smile out of me.

"No, sugar. I'm not an ax murderer—just a rancher with too much work and not enough hands to do it all, who happens to think you're going to like it on my land."

"Sugar?" I scrunched my nose, not sure if I liked being called something so...soft.

"Sugar." He moved closer, brushing against me and sending shock waves of need from the top of my head to the tips of my toes. "Because you smell so damn sweet. I'm wondering if you taste the same as you smell."

Oh my. "I—"

The bus groaned, the engine growing louder as the old behemoth rolled across the parking lot and back onto the highway. Without me on it.

"Shoot," I said, thinking I should be panicked about missing my ride and yet oddly sure I had somehow ended up right where I was meant to be.

"Looks like the decision's been made for you," Liam said, his mouth curling into a self-satisfied sort of smile and looking far too pleased with himself. "C'mon, sugar. Let me take you home with me. I promise, if you end up not wanting what the Hidden E has to offer, I'll put you on the next bus out of town."

Considering what I'd been running from, Liam's offer wasn't the worst option available. So long as he didn't turn out to be as violent as my ex, I figured my fox and I would be okay. Somehow, someway.

And if not, I'd make sure to use that ticket and get the hell out of town.

Chapter Two

The land rolled past, beautiful and wide open. So much more space than in the big cities I was used to. A fox could get used to all that room to run. Not that I was thinking about getting used to anything at that point.

But...maybe.

I turned away from the window, letting my eyes dance over the strong arms and hands of the man sitting next to me. "What kind of horses did you say you raise?"

"Friesians."

That took me aback. "Seriously? I expected Quarter Horses or something."

Liam chuckled, the sound almost like a caress. "Because the farm's out here in cow country?"

"Well...yeah."

"We have a few Quarter Horses on property to help us with the cattle we raise, but our main business has more to do with studding out our Friesian stallions. The rest of the ranch is really just for us to have fun with."

"And you want me to cook for you?"

He glanced my way, his smile teasing and his eyes lustful. "I want you to do whatever you're willing to, sugar."

There was that nickname again. "I'm not sure I like you calling me sugar."

"Why not?"

"I'm not soft."

"But you're sweet."

"Maybe. Or maybe I'm bitter. How would you know since you haven't tasted me?"

That...had sounded way different in my head. Not so sexually suggestive, though I wouldn't mind if he took a little nibble. My fox preened, agreeing with me. Ready to see what the big, bad shifter beside me could do. The hussy.

Liam yanked the wheel and pulled over onto the shoulder, making me squeal at the speed of it all. Without a word, he unbuckled his seat belt and dove across the seat. Grabbed me with his strong hands, yanking me into his arms. Pulling me close. Close enough that I could feel his breath across my lips.

"You offering me a taste, sugar?"

I couldn't breathe. Okay, I could. But it was damn hard. As was the man basically lying on top of me. "Maybe. Why? You want one?"

He shook his head all slow, not breaking our gaze. "One would never be enough."

I thought for sure he was going to kiss me. In fact, I hoped for it. Instead, he sighed and pulled away, squeezing my thigh once as if sad to let me go. "I need to get you to the ranch."

Not really what I wanted to hear, but I conceded. Letting him move back across the seat to his side of the truck. Accepting his retreat...for the moment.

Still, the drive was beautiful and the view inside the cab of his truck better. Even my fox came out of hiding to watch Liam. The tendons in his arms flexed every time he turned the steering wheel, and the solid muscle of his thighs seemed to want to bust out of his jeans. Broad shoulders, thick biceps, and a strong, square jaw made for quite the specimen of masculinity. Something that appealed to both sides of me—

the human and the animal. I could have watched him drive that truck all day.

The trip didn't last that long, though. Soon enough, he turned onto a dirt driveway leading to a cute, ranch-style home with a deep front porch and a big barn out back.

"This is nice," I said as Liam shut off the engine.

"Thanks. Wait right there for me." He hopped out and raced around the front of the truck, rushing to open my door. He even offered me a hand as I climbed down. And if his eyes darted to watch the way my skirt flirted with my upper thighs as I dropped to the ground, well...I didn't mind. At all.

"Such a gentleman. That's not something a girl comes across much anymore." Not much at all from my experience.

Liam brought my hand to his mouth, kissing the back before shooting me a wink and grinning. "We aim to please."

Oh, that smile. It killed me every time. One word caught my attention, though. Had me cocking my head as I asked, "We?"

Before he could answer, three men walked out of the house, all staring my way. All just as gorgeous as the one still holding my hand. Dark hair, light eyes, and big bodies, lined up in a row behind the porch railing.

"Oh...*we.*" Four men on the ranch. And me.

Liam squeezed my fingers and tugged me along beside him. "Come meet my team. I have a feeling they're going to be as enamored of you as I am."

Enamored. We'd only just met, and he already felt enamored. He sounded just like a shifter who'd found his mate, and yet...I didn't feel what I'd always thought I would. I didn't know what I felt. Attraction, sure. In spades, really. Desire, absolutely. But that deep pull on my soul to my one true mate? Not really. *So* confusing.

As we approached the porch, my fox slinked farther out of her hiding spot, watching the men with interest. As soon as she caught their scents —all shifters for sure, none foxes—she chattered loud and strong. She wanted them all. Wanted to sneak away with them and run her bushy tail over their skin.

"Liam," I whispered, gripping his hand tight. Hanging on for dear life as the world spun around me.

"I've got you, sugar. Just trust me."

Trust. Right. Not the easiest thing in the world to give anymore, but I still followed him. Still took the step up into the shade. Damn near stopped breathing as the energy of these guys swept over me. The pull to the men, the gut-clenching need to be around *all four* of them, increased when we came together on that porch. My instincts to claim and mate flared bright. Still, something felt off. The drive to join seemed incomplete somehow, but stronger. So much stronger.

The men definitely seemed to feel the same. They watched me ravenously, four sets of blue eyes taking in every detail. My nipples hardened under their intense stares, and my pussy throbbed, lust stronger than I'd ever experienced before washing over me as I stood before them. Stronger than when I'd met Liam. Stronger than anything I'd ever even heard of. At least, in the fox shifter world. There were other stories, of course. Other breeds of shifters with different histories and cultures. Some of them even took more than one mate, but four?

"Boys, meet Waverley." Liam placed his hand on my lower back and propelled me forward, throwing me to the wolves, it seemed. Or not wolves, as I'd already figured out. "If my sense of smell is correct, she's a fox shifter. And I do believe she's the mate we've been waiting so long for. Where are the others?"

Oh hell.

Chapter Three

Seven. There were seven men total on the farm. Well, not men. Not wholly men. Horse shifters. Stallions. A herd of strapping, handsome men all with dark, wavy hair and eyes in various shades of blue. All ready to claim me as their mate.

My brain couldn't rationalize that thought even as my body responded to the pull to them. The full, legendary mating pull I'd heard about my entire life. The one that left me aroused and needy in all sorts of fun ways, that made my heart race and my legs shake with pure desire. The stallions were definitely fated to be mine.

But...*seven?*

"So, you're saying each one of you would..."

"Fuck you? Absolutely," Matthew, a sharper, cockier version of Liam said with a sarcastic sort of expression on his pretty face. Bad boy. Definitely a bad boy, that one.

Liam smacked him upside the head as he resettled at the kitchen table where we'd been talking for what seemed like a damn lifetime. "Mind your mouth."

"I'd rather she mind it for me."

Liam glared and Garrett chuckled, but Matthew didn't seem to give a single fuck. Definitely the bad boy of the group. Liam appeared to be the leader, the one setting the rules and making sure things stayed balanced. Garrett had already gotten me a snack and something to drink, so I took him as the sweet one. The caretaker. Quinn…well, Quinn had been quiet, watching me from behind a pair of thick, black glasses that made me want to play out a naughty teacher fantasy with him. Tripp was big, jovial, and wore an old football jersey from some college I didn't recognize the name of. Definitely the jock of the group. Dalton and Cade both seemed harder, meaner. Rougher around the edges. While Matthew may have been arrogant and harsher than Liam, those two took that to a whole other level. Something about them spoke of military training or law enforcement. I would bet all the money I didn't have that they were the protectors of the herd.

Easy enough to tell them apart—not so easy to know what to do with them. Or rather, how. Or maybe just what.

Seven. Men.

"Sugar," Liam said, leaning forward and reaching for my hand. "Ask us whatever you need to. I know this sort of thing isn't common, even in the shifter world."

No kidding. "I just…how could there not be fights? Fox shifters mate once and are very territorial about their partners. If another male fox even touched a mated female, there'd be bloodshed."

"Oh, horses are just as territorial," Quinn said, giving me a smile that made my core go liquid. "Trust me, if any male outside the herd came sniffing around, we'd take care of them."

Pictures raced through my head, memories from the night my ex had broken in to my apartment. Had demanded I stay with him. The night he'd nearly killed my male neighbor who'd tried to protect me. All the dead bodies that had piled up afterward. I didn't want to bring that on anyone else again, so Quinn's words were not exactly calming.

But I had to push all that away. I'd escaped, and everything I'd gone through to do so could be talked about and dealt with later. My first concern—my very first consideration on the ranch—had to be in regard to the established herd they had. And how my presence could destroy it.

"I just don't know what I should do here," I said, nearly buckling under the weight of the frowns and disappointed glances thrown my way.

"I'm…I'm really confused by all of this. It's just not how mating works where I'm from."

Liam and Matthew exchanged a look, a long stare where I had a feeling a full conversation happened. Quinn pulled out a tablet and began typing away, looking up at me every few seconds while Dalton watched over his shoulder. And Garrett? He just looked sad.

"You don't want to stay?" Garrett asked.

His pouty lips almost broke my heart. "I don't know. It's a lot to take in."

"She's right," Liam said, rising to his feet. "Waverley needs time to get to know us and to wrap her head around the concept of mating with a herd instead of just one man. She's never even been around horse shifters before." His lips quirked, a smile seemingly trying to fight its way out. "Perhaps we should take a few days and show her what her life could be like with us. Let her fox get the lay of the land and a good look at our stallions."

"Right." Matthew leaned back in his chair, looking positively devilish. "Liam said he bought you a bus ticket in case you wanted to leave, so that gives us what…five days? Plenty of time to introduce this shy little bunny to our way of life. We'll start with a full dinner tonight—all of us together."

"I'm a fox, not a bunny."

He grinned. "Could have fooled me."

"So we're on for dinner." Liam came up behind me, rubbing my shoulders and leaning down close to whisper in my ear. "And maybe, if I'm a real good boy, you'll let me have a little dessert, sugar."

Oh my. I clamped my legs together, hoping like hell the rest of the men couldn't tell how his words affected me. How wet I'd suddenly become or how hard my nipples were beneath my thin, cotton dress. I'd never been so lucky, though. Garrett snorted a laugh, and Matthew looked downright brash. They knew. And if the heated stares they all sent me were any indication, they liked it.

Liked how aroused I got around them.

Liked their chances of convincing me to stay.

Chapter Four

I spent the rest of the day exploring the farm with Liam. He kept the others away, giving me time to get to know just him. To get used to his touch too. The man was handsy, but I liked it. Loved it, really. Soft brushes of his fingers against my hands, a pat to my ass as I walked in front of him, the comfort of his arm around my shoulders. All amazing and so very confusing at the same time. How could he want to touch me so much but be willing to hand me off to another man? And how could I want that? Want to be with him while still thinking about the others? I didn't understand.

Thankfully, Liam never pushed me to try. Instead, he kept up a calm and comforting stream of conversation as we strolled from pasture to woods, from outbuilding to barn. He showed me where their horses lived, where they were bred, where the men worked in their respective roles. He showed me the entirety of the Hidden E Ranch.

I'd never been on such a piece of property—so rural and sprawling. Having lived mainly in cities and suburbs, I knew the idea that acres upon acres of land lay around me with no other humans to be found probably should have made me antsy. Instead, I found myself enjoying the quiet and the peace, wanting to run through the fields and explore.

The open land soothed something inside of me. So did Liam's quiet presence, but he wasn't the only man on the farm. Something I needed to remember.

So as evening began to fall, I asked him to take me back to the house so I could make the boys dinner.

"You don't have to cook," Liam said, even though I could practically see the hunger in his eyes. Hunger for something outside of my body.

"You said you needed a cook, and I'm not afraid to earn my keep. Just give me a little time, and I'll make sure your mouth is watering."

With a growl befitting a wolf more than a stallion, he yanked me off my feet and into his arms, nuzzling my neck before placing a small, wet kiss on my collarbone. "It's been watering since I first saw you, sugar."

Oh, my sexy, charming Liam. I ran my hands through his wavy hair and over his neck, enjoying the moment of connection. The affection he gave so freely. Even my fox sighed and curled up in my mind, comfortable with Liam's presence. Basking in the scent of her mate... One of her seven mates, actually.

I focused on her as Liam held me, trying to discern her instincts on the matter at hand. On the seven. Her response was a quick snort and a sound much like a purr. Or a chuckle. Maybe a laugh. Whatever the noise, the thought of being mated to so many men didn't seem to bother her nearly as much as it did me. In fact, she seemed almost excited to begin the mating process. Still a hussy.

My human side wasn't much better, though. I couldn't help but think what it would be like—the sex, that is. My seven mates were gorgeous in their own ways, all dark-haired with light eyes. All with slightly different builds and features. Would they take me one at a time? All together? Would some watch as a single man took his turn inside me? And oh my stars, why did the thought of *that* turn me on so much?

Liam must have noticed something—a deeper scent or the way my breathing picked up as I imagined him with his face planted between my thighs as my naughty Matthew looked on. Liam seemed to like whatever he sensed, and he definitely reacted. He groaned and ran his hands down my back, gripping my ass and dragging my legs around him. Rubbing hard and pulling me in tight. The solid ridge of his erection rode over my most sensitive spots, the thin cotton and thicker denim between us no match for the heat of me. The wetness. I wanted him, that much I was sure about. But I wanted the others too.

Shouldn't I only want one?

"Stop thinking so much," Liam said as he kissed my neck before biting down hard enough to make me jolt against him. "You're going to give your poor fox a headache."

"My poor fox seems to be doing just fine. It's me who can't turn off my brain."

Liam set me down and spun me around, wrapping his arms around my body once more as he dipped me. "Then think long and hard about this, Waverley. Because once you're ours? We'll never let you go. Stallions mate for life, and a herd is forever."

He kissed me then, firm and deep and exactly what I needed. His tongue slicked into my mouth, and his strong arms caged me against his bigger body. But before I could pull him closer, before I could try to rub myself against him again and ease the ache between my legs, he brought me back to standing and broke the kiss.

"So your fox likes the thought of having seven stallions at her whim?"

I huffed a laugh, hanging on to his arm as we meandered toward the house once more. "I think my fox is more on board with this mating than I am, actually. She seems awfully comfortable with the idea of the seven-to-one ratio."

"Really? Smart little fox."

I shoved him, accomplishing nothing, but eliciting a smile nonetheless. "You just like the idea of getting under my fur."

"Like? No. I love the idea of getting under your fur." He shot me a quick wink before growing serious once more. "Honestly, sugar. What can we do to calm your fears? What worries you so much about this? I know you feel the connection between us." He placed my hand against his chest, turning me to face him and staring down into my eyes. "You feel *me*, don't you?"

The tension between us increased, the need to connect with him almost overwhelming. Almost. "I do. I feel that pull between us, but it's not what I've been expecting, I guess."

He frowned. "Why not?"

"Because I feel it for the others too. Yet it's not all the same—the strength of it varies from one man to the next." I shook my head, unable not to ask the question that seemed to dominate my worries. "Shouldn't I feel the same pull to each of you?"

"Not necessarily, and certainly not right away. The bonds will only strengthen as we all get to know one another better. They'll balance out eventually and become more even, though you'll always feel connected to us in different ways."

"How so?"

"Well, you might come to me for comfort and Matthew for more... shall we say, stimulation." His smile turned downright naughty, something I took to mean he knew exactly how much of a bad boy Matthew could be. "Tripp might be who you joke and play with, while Dalton may be more of a protector. We're all different, so your bonds and your needs for each of us will differ too."

But there was another fear. A deeper one in regard to the seven men. One I was almost too afraid to ask about.

Almost.

"What if I don't end up connected to all of you? What happens to your herd if, say, I only bond with five of the stallions?"

Liam stared down at me for a long moment then shook his head, leading me toward the house with my hand in his. "That's never happened that I know of, but if it does, we'll deal with it as a unit." He paused and licked his lips, looking almost nervous. "None of my guys would ever force you to do something you don't want. Every encounter between us will be on your terms and with your full consent, or it won't happen, if that's what you're worried about."

It wasn't, not really. I already felt attracted to each of them, though in different ways, and I could sense their care for me. I had no fears when it came to my stallions. No sense of danger. I worried more about how each man would handle it when my attention didn't go their way, but I didn't want to say that to Liam right then. I had a feeling he'd tell me everything would be fine, that the guys would behave and accept another male touching their mate. His reassurances would be nice, of course, but I needed to see it, not just hear the words. I needed to know for sure that jealousy between the stallions wouldn't be an issue.

Which was how I concocted my plan for how to handle my first dinner at the Hidden E Ranch.

Chapter Five

Sex and food went hand in hand in my world. So much so that my grandmother had once taught me how to make a beef stew that could appease the hungriest of men in a short amount of time. She used to tell me, "You need something quick to make so you can satisfy your mate in other ways too."

Satiation seemed like the best plan. Perhaps not tonight, though.

Still, I wanted to feed all seven of the men at the table, and they were solid, strapping men. Not a single skinny or lean one among the group. This would require a lot of stew and maybe even some homemade biscuits to fill them up. Plus dessert. Always dessert.

"You don't have to work so hard," Garrett said as he came up behind me and grabbed me around the waist. "We already like you, foxy."

I squeaked as he lifted me off the floor and spun me around, laughing at his antics. But when he set me back on my feet, I caught Liam watching us. At first, I worried his intense stare indicated he was angry or upset, but his smile betrayed that thought. He looked almost...relieved.

"Yeah, c'mon, bunny." Matthew pushed Garrett out of the way and gave my ass a hearty smack. "We'd happily lay you out on the table and have you for dinner. Much less work on your part."

"All right, you two." Liam moved closer, his loose-hipped gait making my mouth water even as Matthew massaged my still-burning ass cheek. Handsy, the lot of them. "The woman wants to cook for us. Considering how bad Dalton has been botching up the job as herd chef, I think we should let her."

"I don't even like to eat *my own* cooking." Dalton stalked into the kitchen, looking at me as if I was what was to be served for dinner. Which apparently seemed to be a theme with these guys. All of them joked about eating me, a thought that led my imagination to those images of Liam's head between my legs as others watched.

I needed some space to cool down.

"Give me forty-five minutes, and I'll have dinner on the table."

My stallions backed off but didn't leave the room. Instead, all seven of them crowded around the table, conversing softly, laughing occasionally, and generally behaving like any other group of men. They just happened to be a group I might someday be having sex with. All seven men. In my bed.

Seriously, it had to be a thousand degrees in the kitchen.

A warm, rough hand grabbed my own, stopping the shaking I hadn't even noticed.

"What can I do to help?" Garrett had come to save the day, looking so sweet and concerned. A real charmer, that one. And obviously in tune with me if he'd noticed me falling apart from across the room.

"Maybe...can you find me some shortening? I need to get the biscuits started."

"Of course." He squeezed my hand once more and smiled down at me before disappearing into the pantry.

Liam took his place at my side. "You okay there, sugar?"

"Yeah." I waved a towel in front of my face. "Just a little warm in here, I guess."

He hummed, looking as if he didn't believe me. That expression, the obvious concern for me, made my fox rush forward. She took control, causing me to chatter softly as I curled into Liam's chest. As I grabbed him and pulled him close, scenting him. Pressing my body against his before she finally relaxed once more and let me lead. But I was awfully happy where I stood, so I held on tighter. Giving Liam the chance to wrap his arms around me and hold me close. No more chattering escaped from me, but my sigh seemed endless.

Liam rocked me slightly, laying his cheek on top of my head and letting me be quiet for a few moments. Allowing me to resettle as my body grew accustomed to his. As his scent soothed my frazzled nerves. Bliss. Mated bliss. Something I'd been waiting for my entire adult life.

"Found the shortening." Garrett appeared beside us, looking concerned. "Everything okay?"

"I think she and her fox needed a bit of support." Liam pulled away, directing me to Garrett. "Why don't you take over for me here? Maybe help her finish up so she can sit and eat with us."

"Of course." Garrett wrapped an arm around my waist, pulling me against his side. Letting me snuggle into his chest the way I had with Liam. His scent was just as soothing, his touch just as calming. The mated bliss just as strong. And Liam? He simply smiled at the two of us and headed back to the table, completely unaffected by the affection between Garrett and me.

Because you mate the herd, not the man. My fox yipped, enjoying every second of being the center of attention for these men. Me? I couldn't quite get past my doubts, no matter how good each man made me feel.

"C'mon, beautiful," Garrett said, guiding me toward the counter where I had the rest of the supplies to make the biscuit dough. "Show me what to do, and I'll help you get dinner finished."

But something still felt off, and I couldn't let it go.

"How do you do it?" I grabbed the flour, unable to look at him. I couldn't even speak the words loudly enough to be sure he heard me. "How could you all possibly learn to share something so...important?"

He huffed, looking completely serious. "It's what we do. We're a herd, a single unit. A family, you know? I want what's best for them, and they want what's best for me. When it comes to a mate, we all want someone who can fit with the entire herd."

"But...I mean...you have to..."

I didn't even know how to say what I wanted to. But Garrett knew. Of course, he did. He leaned close, whispering in my ear so the others wouldn't hear.

"You want to know how I could be happy if you were in my bed one afternoon and Liam's that night? If I went to finger your soft, hot cunt and felt another stallion's come on your thighs?"

Two in one day? I couldn't tell if I was more shocked or turned on by the thought.

"Yeah," I squeaked, sounding more like my animal form than usual. "I just can't see it."

"Because you've never experienced it." He leaned closer, his warm breath fanning across my face and his hand coming to rest on my waist. Pulling me into him. Against him. Letting me feel how hard he was...for me.

"We're close, we stallions. Closer than most shifter groups. If you dropped to your knees for Matthew right now, the rest of us would be thrilled that he was gifted the pleasure of your mouth on him. And if you let me spread you out on the table, allowed me to lick and suck and lavish that pretty pussy of yours with my attention for the next few hours? If you gave me the chance to tease your little clit and taste every inch of you while fucking you with my fingers?" He ran a finger down my thigh, chuckling when I shivered. "Well, every guy at that table would cheer me on, would offer up suggestions and critique, making sure I did it right. That I gave you every bit of pleasure possible so we'd have a sated mate. They wouldn't get mad or jealous that I was the one blessed with the opportunity to eat you out right there in front of them. They'd be watching as you came all over my face for hints on how to please you. That's all every one of us wants—your pleasure. All day, every day."

Oh.

My.

Stars.

My knees shook, and I couldn't catch my breath. The thought of that, of being laid on the table and serviced by one while the rest watched? Maybe even two? Maybe more? Just the possibility was enough to make me want to come right there in the middle of the kitchen. Make me soak my panties as my pussy clenched on nothing.

"Oh," I said, unable to form any more words. Needing to hang on to him to stay standing as heat licked up and down my body.

"*Oh*, indeed." He leaned closer, dropping his voice even more. "I can smell how aroused you are, beautiful. Every man in this room can, and they're all just sitting there enjoying it. Knowing eventually, they'll get to taste that from the source. To have all that heat and slickness wrapped around their tongue or fingers or cock as you come all over them." Garrett chuckled again as I moaned. "Now, let me help you make these biscuits. Good food would bring us all so much pleasure tonight. You want to bring us pleasure, right?"

Yes. Very much so. But words seemed impossible, so I nodded instead.

"Good. Then let's get to cooking. What can I do?"

So many options, none of which would get dinner on the table any faster. None of which I was quite ready to act out with him. Not just yet. I had a feeling of order inside of me, a need to be with a specific man first. To lavish my attention on Liam before the others. That might have been my fox looking for the strongest male, or it might have been herd hierarchy. Whatever the reason, I knew Garrett wouldn't be the first stallion in my bed, no matter how hot his dirty words made me.

And if I read the heated looks Liam was throwing my way correctly, he knew exactly who I'd be coming to first. Or coming with.

Chapter Six

That evening, I stood on the porch looking out over the pastures. My men had spoiled me after dinner, complimenting me for my simple meal and then pampering me with shoulder and foot massages. At least three of them did—the other four had cleaned the kitchen and washed the dishes. Watching them may as well have been a dream come true, especially once they'd removed their shirts and tossed towels over their shoulders for easier drying.

An actual fantasy come to life.

But all good things eventually came to an end, which was how I found myself standing outside on the porch all alone. Not that I minded the quiet—especially not with the view laid out before me. The sun had almost disappeared below the horizon, the last bit of golden light touching the treetops. The gloaming, my grandma would have called it. Such a funny word for such a beautiful hour.

My fox stretched and pawed at my mind, wanting free. Needing to run. The guys were all inside moving furniture around in what had been the guest room. Liam had said it was to give me a private place to sleep in case I wanted my own bed. A thought I was finding more and more unlikely as the time passed. Why sleep alone when I could cuddle with one of my handsome stallions?

Still, a jaunt through the woods sounded good. A chance to let my inner animal out and stretch our muscles. I hadn't shifted much since I'd been on the run, too afraid of the humans around me to risk it. Too terrified of being caught. But if the guys felt safe enough out here in the middle of nowhere to shift into *horses*—something I was dying to see—I could shift into my little fox.

So I did, and it felt just as good as I'd expected it might.

Once firmly standing on four feet, I leaped from the porch and took off at a full run, pumping my legs as fast as I could. Letting the wind ruffle my fur and the hard ground assault my paws. Every ache, every burn of strain, reminded me that I was alive and free still. Able to make my own decisions and choose my own destiny. Fate could push, but in the end, only I could accept or deny her suggestions. I could go anywhere, do anything I wanted...even stay on the Hidden E with my seven mates and live a life I'd never known possible.

That idea had my fox howling, chattering into the evening with her bark-like mating call. I'd called her a hussy for wanting all seven men, but she wasn't the only side of us craving a man's touch. As she ran, focusing on the muscle memory and the instincts that ruled her, I thought about our stallions. About Garrett's dirty words and Matthew's wicked smiles. About Cade and Dalton and how they both looked at me with such intensity. Quinn and Tripp, both almost strangers still, and yet not. About Liam and all the naughty things I wanted to do to him. About how I craved him in my bed and my body first.

As if I'd somehow called for one of my men, a tall, strong-looking horse came racing into the field in front of me. A stallion shifter for sure. Head high and back arched, he looked like some sort of mythical beast come to rescue his woman from whatever distressed her. The only thing that distressed me, though, was the need making my entire body quake.

The horse snorted, pawing at the ground as he watched me. His thick neck was covered by a shiny mane, the waves coming all the way down to his broad chest. His tail hung to his hooves, and every single inch of him was as black as night. Any later in the evening and I wouldn't have been able to see him at all. That would have been a pity.

But a fox and a horse couldn't do much in terms of slaking the need building inside of me, so I shifted to my human form. My pale skin replaced my red fur, and I moved from four feet to two. Rose to my full height and stood watching the commanding beast. Naked. Fully, unabashedly naked. I only had a second to question that fact—to wonder if I lived up to his expectations of feminine beauty. If my wide hips, heavy thighs, and big boobs were attractive or a turn-off. Foxes liked sweets—candies, cakes, and cookies. There was no getting around that, and my body reflected it. Thankfully, my stallion didn't seem to mind.

He approached me slowly, keeping his head down and his eyes on mine until he stood close enough to touch. His muzzle felt as soft as velvet when I reached a hand for it, his breath warm. He sniffed all over me, flipping his lip against my skin as if trying to taste me. From my shoulders to my knees, even brushing across my hip bones. He left nothing out. I mimicked him but with my hands. Rubbing, touching, working the tips of my fingers over his neck and shoulders, across his face and up over his forelock. Such a beautiful animal. Such a strong creature. Every inch of him seemed to be covered in thick, heavy muscles, just like my men. But something about the look in his eyes, something about the attraction I felt for him, let me know exactly who I was dealing with.

And it was time to truly deal with him.

"Shift, Liam. Be a good mate and give me what we both want."

Almost instantly, human Liam stood before me. Just as naked as I was. Just as aroused, as well. His rippled abs led down to a sturdy and erect cock, one that stood thick and long and practically purple with his need. He gripped it tightly with one hand, breathing hard and watching me with that deep, dark gaze of his. Tugging roughly as I stared. Stroking himself right there in front of me.

"Look what you do to me, sugar." Liam squeezed his cock tighter, his arm moving faster. "Look how hard you make me. I'm dripping for you, and you haven't even touched me yet."

Unable to resist, I reached for him, running my fingers over the head of his cock as his fist moved down the length of it. He shivered and groaned, looking ready to eat me up. Ready to lay me down right there in the grass.

And I was ready to let him.

"I want this to work," I said, keeping my voice low and soft. Pressing my body to his and running my nose along his neck. "I'm willing to try, at least."

His hands landed on my waist, yanking me against him as he rolled his hips into mine. As he trapped his cock between us and pushed it against the front of my pussy. "That's all I can ask for. A chance. Let me introduce you to how good it can be to be mated to a stallion, my little fox. Let me be the one to give you pleasure tonight."

I nodded, moaning as his lips found mine. As his hands slid over my ass to the backs of my thighs and lifted me off the ground. I wrapped my legs around his waist and held on as he laid me down right there in the field. Grasses and clover softened my descent, cool and silky against my skin. But my Liam? He was all hot and hard, his hands roughened from the work he did and his lips overpowering against mine. So strong and virile, so sexy and masculine. So perfect.

He broke the kiss to move his cruel mouth down my body, biting at my neck while teasing my nipples with his fingertips. Pinching and making me gasp. Twirling and making me moan. His cock sat against my thigh, heavy and hard, leaving a wet spot that only made me want him more. Made me want *this* more. Because the time had come for our first mating. The feelings inside of me—the ones solely focused on Liam in that moment—could only be the intense lust I'd always heard about when two mates came together. There would be no denying it, no stopping. There was nothing in our way. Only us. Only our wants and needs playing out under the stars.

"May I?" Liam asked as he knelt between my thighs, licking his lips and looking down to where my knees had splayed. To where my pussy sat on display. For him. All for him.

I nodded, unable to speak, too turned on to do anything more than spread my legs wider to give him room. He took my invitation, dropping down to wedge his shoulders between my thighs. His breath made me shiver, made my pussy clench on nothing as he came closer and closer and...

Oh.

My.

Stars.

His tongue killed me from the first swipe. Hot and wet, almost violent in its strength. He lapped at me, licking around my clit before flattening out and stroking all the way up my slit. I yelped into the night, my back arching as sensations rocketed up my spine and down through my toes. As every nerve fired at once, all converging right there beneath his tongue.

Liam held me down and dove in again, licking, sucking, biting, teasing. Driving me right to the edge and backing off, lapping at every drop of my arousal as I writhed and yelled nonsense into the emptiness of the world around us.

"Just as sweet as I thought," Liam said, his voice a growl. His hands still greedy on my thighs. "Give me every drop, sugar. I want to lick you all up."

He slipped two fingers inside me, pumping hard and fast. Working my pussy like a man possessed, like he had a mission to make me come as fast and strong as possible. And I submitted to him—my body bending to his will without question. This surrender, this all-out need to let him have his way with me, was what I'd wanted since I saw him standing in that parking lot, baking under the sun. This was what I'd needed all day.

First his mouth and fingers, then his cock. A triple play to remember.

I bit back another yelp as he wrapped his lips around my clit and sucked, teasing me with the tip of his tongue even as his fingers pressed deep. So very deep. Driving me insane with the tightness and the pressure.

His hips rocked against my legs, his body humping the ground as he brought me right to the edge. That tight, round butt of his reflecting the moonlight and stealing every bit of my attention. I wanted to grip it. Grab it. Claw my fingers across it to see the red streaks bloom on the pale flesh. Soon. So fucking soon. Once he made it inside me, I could grab him. Hold on as he moved within me. I just had to...just needed to... oh my stars, if he kept sucking that way...

I came with a howl that would have impressed any other foxes in the area. My body shook, my eyes locked closed, and every sense gave itself over to the pleasure that came from Liam's skilled mouth and hands. He didn't stop either. He kept licking and teasing, kept his fingers buried deep inside me as I pulsed and rocked and clenched and soaked him. As I came harder than I ever had before.

"More?" Liam asked as he worked his way up my body once I'd finally stopped shaking. "Let me give you more, sugar. Let me give you all of me. You're good and wet right now. I bet you're tight, though. Bet I'll still have to work my thick cock inside your little pussy even though you're so soaked. Tell me you want everything, and I'll give it to you. Every inch of my everything."

Oh, his cock. He wanted to give me his cock. And good gravy, did I want to have every inch of it. I nodded my consent, reaching for his shoulders and dragging him up to my mouth so I could steal a kiss. He tasted like me, a fact that had me moaning and sliding my tongue into his mouth for more. Liam acquiesced, thrusting his tongue against mine even as he reached between us to line up his thick cock with where I was so fucking drenched for him. Where I was already so swollen and tight.

I had to break the kiss when he pushed forward, the girth of the man stretching me almost to the point of pain. Making me keen and pull my legs up toward my chest so I could open myself more for him.

"Oh, my stallion." I arched my back and rolled my hips, wanting to retreat but needing more of him at the same time. So full, so full. Every inch pulling, every muscle tense but yielding.

Liam stayed slow and patient, working his way inside. Rolling his body over mine as his cock moved back and forth inside me, as he groaned and grunted with the strain of going easy on me. And his face— so hard and focused. Completely set on his task. On taking care of me like a good mate should.

But I wanted him to *fuck* me.

"Harder." I pulled my knees up all the way to his chest, wrapping them as far around him as I could. "I need harder."

"Fuck, sugar. You're too fucking tight. If I pound you like I want to, I'm going to come in about ten seconds. Let me get you off first."

"You already did." I groaned as he slipped deeper, as he punched up into me and made me clench down on him. "Yes, that. I want you deep like that. Deeper still."

"If I get much deeper, I'm going to come. I'll come inside you."

How such simple words could make me grow even wetter, I had no idea. "I want that. Please."

"Yeah?" He pushed harder, staring down at me. Watching as he bottomed out and made me gasp.

"Fuck yeah. Like that. All the way deep."

"You want me balls deep? I knew you were perfect for us. Knew it from the second I saw you. Whatever my little fox wants, she gets." He grunted, driving home a little harder. Rocking me up the grass as his thrusts grew in their power. And when he bottomed out again, when his balls slapped my ass on a brutal thrust, I screamed for him.

"Liam. Yes. That, that, that. Oh god, I need it."

He groaned long and deep as he hammered into me, as I dug my nails into his back and held my knees up against his shoulders.

"Fucking perfect little pussy. So soft and hot, and so damn tight." He pulled almost all the way out then thrust deep again, making me yelp with the intense shock of sensation the move sent shooting through my body. "That's it, sugar. I've got your pussy wrapped all around me, and I'm going to make sure it gets exactly what it deserves. So tight, so tight. Oh fuck, I want to come inside you so bad. Want to fill you up."

He dropped his head to my chest, biting one nipple while he fucked into me. The dual sensations—the two points of slight pain and intense pleasure—made my brain go sideways. There was nothing else, no words to say, no places to move. There was only Liam and his cock inside me, his teeth in my flesh, and my body taking everything he had to give. He muttered words like soft and lush against my skin, panted and groaned and growled as he pushed deeper, changed angles, and pushed deeper again. There was no stopping us, no pausing. Just him and me and fucking ourselves silly right there under the night sky.

"Deeper," I grunted as his strokes lost their controlled rhythm. "Just a little deeper. I want you to come so deep inside me, Liam. Need it."

He nodded, panting, moving faster over me and grunting with every renewed thrust. And by the stars, did the man accomplish his goal. Deep, almost painfully so, he thrust over and over again. Making my entire body seize up as I approached that final cliff. As my pussy quaked and the pressure built within me. As I broke, coming with a scream and clawing at his shoulders as if to hold on to something. To find purchase as I flew through the pleasure of an orgasm too big to see the end of.

Liam followed right behind me, practically roaring as he froze. His hips pressed tight against mine, his cock seated deep inside of me as he filled me with his seed. As he bred me. Because that could happen—I knew it, he knew it, and every other male on this farm knew it. As mates, it didn't matter that we were different breeds. If we fucked, I could get pregnant.

A thought that only made me want to do it all again.

So, we did.

On the second go, Liam flipped me onto my knees and slid inside me from behind. The new angle had me seeing stars and coming faster than before. His fingers pinching my clit certainly helped with that.

By the third time, we'd slowed down. Kissing through every thrust and keeping our bodies connected from shoulders to knees.

And after the fourth time, with me on my side and him rolling his entire body against mine as he scissored my thighs, he picked me up off the grass and kissed my forehead.

"Time to get you to bed, my sweet mate."

I groaned, my body sore but sated. My mind spinning. Bed. His or mine? Ours? Someone else's? I had no idea, but I knew once we got back to the farmhouse, I had a decision to make. A big one.

We'd be walking into a house full of males, all my mates, with Liam's scent all over and inside me. And though I'd chosen Liam to be my first sexual partner, that didn't mean I had to choose him to share a bed with. Sex was one thing. Sleeping arrangements were something entirely different.

And potentially dangerous.

Chapter Seven

Whoever said you can't go home again apparently hadn't been a horse shifter, because Liam had no issues with dragging me back to the ranch house. Thankfully, night had fallen well and good, the darkness blanketing the farm hiding us from any peeping toms. Needing more coverage, we stopped in the barn to grab a couple of cloaks. The simple garments tended to be a staple on any shifter's property because our clothes didn't shift with us. Nakedness while having sex outside? Awesome. Nakedness while running into your elderly neighbor? Not so much.

Matthew met us in the kitchen when we walked inside from our night under the stars. I froze, almost afraid of what was to come. There was no denying what Liam and I had been up to—between the wild hair, the scent of sex covering us, and the fact that we stood naked under the cloaks, we were pretty well busted. Matthew didn't balk, though. In fact, he shot me one hell of a sexy smile as he looked me up and down.

"I'll assume you two had fun." He raised a coffee cup to his lips and took a sip before asking, "My turn next?"

Liam wrapped an arm around my waist, pulling me against him and leaning in so his face sat next to mine. "It's up to Waverley."

I clutched Liam's arm, unsure of the right answer. Did I stay with the man who'd just gotten naked with me out in a field or move on to the next man in line? There were pros and cons for each decision, but my biggest worry had to do with the men's reactions. Would Liam be okay with me heading right into Matthew's bed? And how would Matthew deal with me turning him down to stay with Liam a little longer?

"She's nervous." Matthew set his mug down and moved toward us. "My shy bunny's wondering what the best answer is, am I right?"

I nodded, unable to speak as he sauntered into my space. As his big body pinned me against Liam's. Matthew raised his hand to my face, brushing a single finger along my cheek as he moved to place a soft, chaste kiss against my lips.

"Tell her, Liam," he said. The closeness of him, the way he watched me, made my body respond. Made my legs quake and my nipples harden. And with Liam at my back? So wet.

"The choice is always yours," Liam murmured into my ear, forcing a shiver to erupt in my spine. "You can have us all. Have us however, whenever, and in whatever order you choose. In a herd mating, everything is about making sure our female is happy and completely satisfied. You're in charge here."

Liam moved his hands down my body to my hips. Holding me in place with my ass pressed tight against the hard ridge of his cock. Matthew inched forward, sliding his long body against the length of mine. Keeping his hands up over my waist, holding on to me even as he ran his thumbs against the underside of my breasts. Teasing, as always. Pushing boundaries.

"You're so innocent," Matthew whispered, dropping down to kiss me again, this time a little less chaste. A little longer and deeper. Leaving me moaning when he pulled away. "So sweet and shy, too. I can't wait to spread you out on my bed and make you beg for my cock."

Liam chuckled, his chest rumbling against my back. "Just wait until you make her scream nonsense. Best moment of my life so far, knowing I pushed her to the point of not being able to form words."

Matthew's wandering hands covered my breasts, his fingers and thumbs pinching my nipples hard enough to make me jump. "Are you a screamer, bunny? I never would have guessed that."

There was no way to deny that these two men—*my* men—had me

completely at their mercy. Trapped between them, practically helpless and under their control, I could do nothing but enjoy every second of their attention. Of their touches. Of Matthew's hands massaging my breasts rough and hard. Of Liam's hands sliding down my thighs and between my legs to tease me toward another orgasm. Of their bodies pressed against mine. Such a naughty thing to be doing. Such delightful torture.

"Looks like dinner started without us." Garrett walked into the kitchen from the back entrance with Quinn on his heels. Both men stopped to watch Liam and Matthew overpowering me. Stopped to appreciate the show, if the looks on their faces were any indication. And neither seemed upset in the least that I had two men with their hands all over my body. A fact that turned me on, and yet...

"Liam," I whispered, needing more from him. More support and assurance. More comfort.

"All up to you." He kissed my neck, gripping my thighs tightly. "You choose the who and the when. We'll take care of you. You don't have to stay with me just because I got the first taste of that sweet pussy tonight."

And that was my Liam. A leader at heart, kind and selfless, knowing the one thing I truly needed and giving it to me without reserve.

Control.

"I want each of you," I said, bringing my hands up to Matthew's arms and hanging on. Grounding myself between my current lover and my next one. "Be patient, though. I want to get to know you all as more than just bed partners. I'd like to spend a bit more time with each one of you. Maybe one day and night per mate for now."

"You heard the lady. She's mine for the night." Liam chuckled against my ear and kissed my neck again. "And I fully intend to make you scream nonsense again."

Matthew gave my nipples one last squeeze, leaning in for one last kiss too. He made it a good one, of course. Long and wet, deep and hot. Looking almost wild when he finally broke it. "Until tomorrow, shy bunny."

I could only nod. How did a girl find words when she had a man looking at her the way Matthew looked at me? He didn't need to charm me or even *try* to get between my legs. With a look like the one he threw my way, I'd strip right then and there for him. Let him do whatever he wanted.

But first, I needed a little more time with Liam. And a little time to resettle my nerves before I ended up in bed with my stallion.

Which meant a distraction was in order. "Are you boys hungry? I could make you a snack."

Liam spun me around, leaning in to kiss me before pulling back so his forehead rested against mine. "I'm hungry, sugar. But what I crave doesn't require much preparation." He slid his hands over my ass, dropping lower so he could stroke my pussy from behind. "I plan to eat your cunt the second I get you in my bed, so if you need nourishment to keep going tonight, grab something quick. If you take too long, I'll toss your pretty ass on this table and let the boys watch as I lick up every drop of your sweetness."

I clenched my thighs together, the wetness running down them a sure sign of how his words affected me. This man and his filthy mouth— I couldn't resist them.

"I'm not hungry. At least, not for food." I looked up at him from under my lashes, flashing him a smile as I palmed his thick cock. "But I'd much rather we keep the show private for right now."

"Just us?"

I nodded, biting my lip as I ran my fingers over the head of him. "Just me, you, and this thick cock making me forget my words."

His eyes darkened, his face growing stormy. "Lock up, okay, boys?"

Matthew chuckled from somewhere behind us as Quinn rolled his eyes with a smile on his handsome face, but I paid them no mind. I was getting used to these public declarations. These intimate moments shared with the others. Getting used to them...and maybe even growing to like them. Which was why, when Liam picked me up and threw me over his shoulder, securing me in place with his big hand covering my bare ass, I could do nothing but laugh and wave goodnight to the other men standing around the kitchen.

There was no fear, no shame, and no expectations other than good sex that night. A life impossible to resist.

A reality too good to be true.

Chapter Eight

Waking up in Liam's arms after a long night of him over me, under me, with his face buried between my legs, or with his cock deep in my throat was just about as perfect as I could have imagined. Though, after such a night, I finally understood what that old cowboy saying *rode hard and put away wet* meant. Every part of me hurt, each muscle sore and aching from the strain of the night before. Even the flesh between my legs felt bruised and swollen from the attention it had received.

What an absolutely delightful way to start the day.

While my stallion slept on, I rolled out of his bed and grabbed one of his shirts, trying to be as quiet as possible. The man needed his sleep. He'd been an animal the night before, fucking me relentlessly in his bed, on his floor, and even once in his shower while he'd pressed me up against the tile wall. He'd said he needed to take advantage of every moment we had together if he was going to have to wait a week to get a second chance with me. Something that I would have assumed indicated some sort of jealousy, but the words had been delivered in a simple, truthful, almost excited way. As if he looked forward to what we could do right then and what he could plan for the next time.

Still, I fretted. I was a fretting fox filled with feels. Or something like that.

When I stepped into the kitchen and saw Matthew pulling out eggs and bacon for breakfast, that fretting turned to downright worry. Would he still be okay with everything in the light of day? Seeing me as I was—obviously well-fucked and wearing Liam's shirt? I'd turned Matthew down the night before, and he'd seemed okay with it. But now? Would he—

"I swear, bunny. I can hear you thinking from across the room." Matthew turned, shooting me a devilish smile and crooking a finger at me. "Get your sexy ass over here and help me make some grub before the rest of the boys wake up."

I shuffled across the floor, biting my lip. Still unsure of his feelings about everything, but running on the assumption that he wasn't playing with me. That he felt okay about the decision I'd made the night before. That we would be fine.

If the way he grabbed me around the waist and planted me in front of him was any indication, he was more than just okay. He seemed downright joyful, happy to have his hands on me again. I relaxed into his hold, softening to match his shape. To meet as much of his body with mine as possible. To steal a little comfort from him.

Humming softly, Matthew placed a hand flat on my stomach, holding me still with my ass pressed into his hips—practically using my body to cradle his hard cock.

"I'm not a good cook," he said, his voice low and sultry. Teasing, even. "But I'm good for whatever else you need. All you have to do is ask."

Matthew rocked into me, groaning in my ear as he moved to bite the lobe. My head fell back, that spark of pain igniting something inside of me. Something warm and liquid—a viscous sort of pleasure heating me from the center out. His hands followed my curves along my hips, one sliding down, kneading my flesh along the way, moving until he had his fingers planted firmly against my pussy. Cupping me. Possessing the most intimate part of my body. His other hand moved up, up, up until it could grasp my breast. Palm the heavy flesh with a grip just this side of too hard. He had me pinned against him, his strong, muscled arms locking me in some sort of sexual hold. One I wanted more of. That I could only moan and gasp and curl my body into as my way to ask for more.

But he definitely knew what I needed even without my having to ask. He dragged his fingers along the flesh between my legs, teasing with his touch. Winding me up like a top so he could watch me spin. There was no way he could miss how hot and wet I already was for him. How needy he made me with just a touch.

"Matthew," I whispered as I rocked into his hand. Unable to stop my body from moving.

He chuckled, pressing harder, tweaking my nipple at the same time. "You're going to do exactly what I say, aren't you, bunny? You're going to be such a good girl for me."

I would. I already knew I would because he'd make me. Not hurting, not forcing, just...demanding in that confident way he had. Pushing me to give him whatever he needed. What we both needed. So commanding, my Matthew. So in control. Liam liked to be in control as well, but the two men's styles differed greatly. Liam didn't demand. He led people, guiding them through their choices and giving them the opportunity to make the right decisions. Matthew dominated them. He told people what to do and expected them to follow his orders. Both had the best interests of the ones around them at heart, but Matthew's desires overshadowed anyone else's in his mind. He wanted exactly what he wanted, and he'd get it no matter what.

I couldn't wait to see what he *wanted* to do to me in the bedroom.

"Well now, that's one hell of a sight first thing in the morning." Tripp —the jock of the group—came barreling into the kitchen with a broad smile on his face as he took in Matthew's hold on me. "Morning, doll. Matty. What's for breakfast?"

"Your dick if you keep calling me Matty." Matthew kissed my neck and gave me a good squeeze before turning us toward the crowd quickly assembling. All my men—even Liam—sat around the table. Watching us. I hadn't heard them come in, hadn't noticed they'd joined us as Matthew had groped me at the counter. The kitchen suddenly seemed to be a thousand degrees again.

I needed a distraction.

"Eggs and bacon okay for everyone?" I asked, trying—and failing—to keep my voice from coming out too high. Too fake. Apparently, I had no chill. "I still have some biscuits from last night as well."

Liam nodded, his lips quirking in a satisfied, contented sort of smile. "That'd be great, sugar. We'll be thrilled with whatever you make for us."

"I'll help," Matthew said, moving me aside and nodding toward the ingredients he'd already pulled from the refrigerator. "My hands are yours, bunny. What do you want me to do with them?"

The way his lips turned up into that quintessential Matthew smirk told me he'd planted that double entendre on purpose. And though my body responded to his offer—heart beating harder and pulsing in areas farther south than just my chest—I kept that response as hidden as I could.

"You start the bacon, and I'll get to work on the eggs."

"Your wish is my command." He moved in close, biting the lobe of my ear again before whispering, "For now, at least. Because, tonight in my bed? I'll be the one commanding."

He smacked my ass—way harder than I would have expected—and moved to the counter to open the packets of bacon. I glanced at the table, almost afraid of what I'd see on my men's faces. Instead of anger or irritation, they all seemed truly happy and ready to start the day. Too busy with their own conversations to even notice Matthew manhandling me. Except Liam. He caught me looking, shooting me a lopsided grin as he sat back in his chair. Practically encouraging me with his eyes.

Maybe...just maybe...this crazy thing could work, after all.

Chapter Nine

After a breakfast served with jokes, teasing comments, and lustful stares from Liam and Matthew, my guys headed out to do... whatever it was they did. Each one took the time to say goodbye, offering hugs and kisses and ass-smacks along the way...well, most of them. Quinn nodded my way before saying something about being around the house if I needed him, while Dalton and Cade went straight to the basement. No goodbye, no kiss on the cheek. Nothing.

Their indifference shouldn't have stung as much as it did.

Liam and Matthew made up for their lack of attention, though, both of them kissing me deeply before walking out the door. Matthew even added his signature ass-smack on his way. I wouldn't have expected anything less from him.

I spent the morning cleaning and baking. It gave me something to do, something to focus on as I tried to stop worrying so much. The Hidden E and life with my stallions seemed too good to be true, which meant my mind spun out of control with all the what-ifs and could-happens. What if one of the men decided he didn't want me as a mate? What if someone ended up jealous? What if we all weren't compatible, after all?

What if, what if, what if. Ugh.

I was in the middle of kneading dough to make a few loaves of bread when Matthew came in from outside. His cheeks looked redder than usual, his eyes harder. Even his walk carried more aggression in it as his feet pounded the floors. He seemed dangerous in that moment...and completely focused on me.

"Matthew, what—"

He didn't let me finish; instead, he yanked on my ponytail and pulled my head back until he'd forced me to look straight up at him. I moaned, unable not to. His dominant side spoke to something in me, something deep and buried. Something that made me want to do whatever he said, exactly as he said it—and then not do it, just to see how far he'd go. If he would *make* me.

I really liked the idea of him making me.

"I've been thinking about you all morning, bunny." Matthew pressed his hips against my side, making sure I felt his hardness. Stroking a finger across my lips as he held me in place. "I bet Liam was nice and sweet with you out in that field. Bet he licked that pussy good before he fucked you."

I nearly whimpered, nearly came remembering, too. Matthew's arrogant smile grew as if he knew exactly how much I liked what he was doing to me. And maybe he did—my nipples were hard as stone, even the light fabric of Liam's T-shirt brushing against them too stimulating, and my pussy had already soaked the thin cotton fabric of my panties. There was no way he didn't notice both of those facts.

Though, if he did, he didn't say anything. Instead, he leaned closer, bringing his face right against mine, almost brushing my lips with his as he spoke. "You ready for me yet, my shy bunny? You willing to give me my turn to take care of that pussy?"

So much yes. Too much to say, so I nodded instead. His grin went cocksure, and his hand gripped my face tighter. "Good. Because I've been imagining just how well Liam treated that pussy yesterday. He's a fucking gentleman, that one. But I want to make sure you know something before I take my turn."

He waited, breathing hard. Holding me so I couldn't move. Until I finally broke.

"What do you want me to know?"

His expression turned full-on wicked. "I'm not that fucking nice."

He spun me around and pushed me to the floor, to my knees. His intentions clear, his need obvious behind the fly of his jeans. And I... surrendered. Did exactly what I knew he wanted me to. I reached for his pants and unfastened them. Pulled the heavy denim far enough down his thighs to free his long, hard cock. Wrapped my hand around that steely flesh and directed him to my mouth, opening wide for him. Sucking him deep right from the start. Wanting to be such a good girl. Just for him.

"Good bunny. That's my girl," he said, groaning loud and long as I took him deep. As deep as I could, which wasn't enough. But when I reached to hold the base of his cock, to grip what couldn't fit, he smacked my hand away. "Do you suck cock with your hands, bunny? I don't think so. Take it. Take it all. I know you can do it, so leave those hands on my thighs or use them on yourself. You're not allowed to touch my cock."

Wet. Soaked. Positively dripping. My pussy practically melted right there in the middle of the kitchen, covered in flour, on my knees with Matthew's cock in my mouth. I nearly came without a single bit of direct stimulation, nearly collapsed in a pile of girl on that hard floor because of him. His words, his demands, made me want to please him. Made me want to try harder and push myself to my limits, then blow right past them. Made me want to swallow his cock as far down my throat as I could.

So I tried.

With my hands pressing firmly on his thighs, I sucked him deeper. Looking up at him from under my lashes as I worked to relax my throat and let him inside. He stared down at me with a fire burning in his beautiful blue eyes, his hand fisted in my hair to direct my pace, his hips rocking slightly. Controlled. Which wasn't what I wanted.

I wanted him to lose that tight hold on himself. I wanted him wild, wanted him to fuck my face and make me gag on his length. Wanted him to come down my throat and tell me how well I'd done. I wanted him to use me for his pleasure.

I squeezed his thighs, digging my nails into his flesh as I bobbed on his length. Pushing him as hard as he pushed me. Moaning with every sign that he had lost a bit more control. And he did lose it—rocking, thrusting, growling more and more. Faster with every minute that passed, harder with every shove into my mouth. He used me well, groaning when he finally slipped into my throat and I almost—*almost*—had him completely inside my mouth.

"Look at you, my good little bunny. So open for me." He adjusted his grip on my hair, pulling me harder against him. "You going to let me come in that naughty little mouth of yours? You going to swallow down all my come and beg for more? I bet you will. I fucking *bet* it. Christ, your mouth is a fucking dream."

He groaned, his eyes slipping closed as he pushed deep enough that my nose ended up buried against the flesh of his abdomen. I nearly gagged, my mouth watering like crazy and tears coming to my eyes, but I held myself together. I let him fuck my mouth, allowed him to slide that long, thick cock as far down my throat as he needed to. I relaxed into the act and took every bit of him that I could.

And I loved it. As did he.

"Fuck, bunny. Fuck. Your mouth. It's...it's too much. Too good." He groaned and pressed deep, coming down my throat, his entire body arching toward me as he gave himself over to his orgasm.

I swallowed around him, not wanting to spill a drop. Not wanting to disappoint him. I never took my eyes off his face either. He looked so beautiful in his release—so animal and wild, so feral. I wanted to see that expression again, wanted to make him lose that control he loved so much. And though I would be shared with the other men of the herd, I wanted to keep him to myself. Wanted to be the only one ever to see the face he made as he came.

I wanted him to be wholly mine. Just like the rest of my stallions.

Chapter Ten

"Y"ou okay, Waverley? You seem a little flushed."

I ducked my head, avoiding Quinn's inquisitive gaze as I fidgeted in Matthew's lap. "I'm fine, thanks. It just got a little hot in here earlier. Warm. Because of the oven. Want another biscuit?"

Matthew choked on a laugh, the asshole. Ever since the other stallions had made their way inside for a late lunch, he'd been teasing me. Little touches and pinches, naughty words spoken just to get a rise out of me. Constant attention to my mouth.

The others seemed to have picked up on his obsession too. They all appeared to be trying to push my buttons. To make me blush. To make sure I knew that *they knew* exactly what I'd been doing when I should have been cooking.

I was going to smack each and every one of them if they kept it up.

"You know who likes biscuits?" asked Tripp, biting back a grin. "Matthew. He'd probably drop to his knees and beg—"

"Stop it," I snapped. My fox tucked herself into a corner of my mind, hiding. Avoiding the ire running through me. Smart girl. "If you all don't stop teasing me, Matthew will be the only one of my mates who ever has a 'drop to my knees' moment with me."

Six men shut up quick, but one—Matthew, *of course*—sat back with a smirk.

"You too, mister," I said, leveling a glare at him. "You keep egging them on, and that will be the last time I...do that."

His smile grew more devilish as he leaned forward. "Do what, bunny? Why, I was just sitting here enjoying this delicious lunch you made for us. I have no idea what all the hubbub is about. Why don't you tell me what it is you're threatening to deny me?"

If looks could kill, he'd be toast. As would the cocky grin on his face.

"You know," Garrett said, sitting back and raising an eyebrow at Matthew. "If Matthew's not making you happy, you can always come spend the night with me, beautiful. I'd be happy to do whatever I can to put you in a better mood."

Liam smirked. "Or you could come spend the evening with me out in the pasture, sugar. I'll put a smile on your face."

"You two are assholes," Matthew said, scowling.

I raised an eyebrow. "Assholes who apparently want to see me happy."

He frowned. "You think I don't want to see you happy?"

"It's hard to tell." I shrugged one shoulder, smiling across the table at a grinning Liam. "I mean, Liam was such a giver. And you...not so much."

Matthew suddenly picked me up and rose to his feet before plopping me into the chair he'd just left. He stalked to the refrigerator, his steps hard and a heavy scowl on his face. A man on a mission—one whom I'd pissed off, apparently. With sharp movements, he opened the appliance door and reached inside. I glanced at Liam, who shook his head and went back to watching the other stallion, his heavy brow furrowed in confusion. Apparently, I wasn't the only one who had no idea what was coming.

Matthew slammed the refrigerator door closed, recapturing my attention. Without pausing, he headed back to the table, a white box in his hand and an angry expression on his pretty face.

He tossed the box in front of me. "Open it."

I stared up at him, uncomfortable with his anger. Unsure of whether I wanted to listen to him or if I should run. If I should escape. He must have sensed my discomfort because he sighed and softened his voice.

"Please. Open it."

With a glance around the table, I did as he asked, untying the simple string around the box and lifting the top. My fox nearly fell over when she scented the contents, and I moaned.

"What is it?" asked Quinn, stretching to see inside.

I pulled the box against my chest. The *bakery* box. "It's mine, that's what it is."

Matthew leaned over my shoulder, his voice like rough asphalt as he whispered, "Did I do well, bunny?"

I nodded and reached into the box, pulling out a small, perfectly gorgeous little tart. Crystallized sugar clung to the top, decorating the dark red fruit center like snow. So pretty, so sweet, and so going in my mouth. "Where did you get them?"

"I drove out to Fairview. Figured the best place to find the perfect treats for my little fox was a fox sanctuary." He frowned at the box. "The whole town smelled like a bakery."

Fairview. My original destination. But that was so far. "When did you have time to drive there? That's like...four hours away."

I bit into the tart and moaned. Sweet, delicious. And so damn addictive.

"Five. It's five hours. And I didn't go today but last night." He smiled, his eyes heated as he ran a finger over my cheek. "When you came into the kitchen this morning, I'd just gotten back."

Oh. *Ooooooooh.* My dominating stallion had a sweet side.

"You stayed up all night to bring me these?"

He shot me that cocky smile. "Still think I'm not a giver?"

I was up and out of my seat in a heartbeat, had my arms wrapped around his neck in another. And then I kissed him, rose onto the balls of my feet and pressed my lips to his. Slid my tongue against his as soon as he allowed me inside. I kissed him to make myself happy—taking from him. Stealing a moment that made him groan.

"Thank you," I said when I finally pulled away. "These are just what I needed."

"Yeah?" He licked his lips, staring down at my mouth. "Pick a couple that you want to take with you."

"Where am I going?"

"To my room." He leaned closer and dropped his voice nice and low, letting it slide all over me like hot fudge over ice cream. "All that sugar made your mouth taste sweet. I want to see if that sugary goodness is just as strong on other parts of you."

My breath caught, and the fiery look in his eyes made my pussy clench. "Yeah?"

He nodded, moving closer to place a soft, promising kiss on my upturned lips.

"You two get everything settled?" Liam asked, raising an eyebrow in our direction when we broke apart.

I nodded, grabbing two of the tarts and handing the box back to Matthew so he could return it to the refrigerator. Those pastries were not to be wasted. "We're good. But we're going to go now, and I'm going to be keeping him busy the rest of the day."

Tripp cocked his head, grinning. "What are you going to be doing, doll?"

To be honest or to hide? That was the question. I looked to Matthew. He shrugged, letting me decide what to say. These men, my mates, had teased me horribly about sucking Matthew's cock. Meanwhile, Matthew himself had stayed up all night to bring me pastries he knew I'd like. If anyone deserved a reward, it was my dominant mate.

So I tossed my hair over my shoulder and grabbed Matthew's hand as soon as he'd made his way back to me.

"I'm taking Matthew to his room. I think he deserves a nice, long ride for bringing his mate such delectable treats." I shot Matthew what I hoped was a lascivious grin. "And if he's really good, I might even allow him to lick my pretty cunt."

He raised an eyebrow. "Allow me? Just try to stop me, bunny."

Yeah. That wouldn't be happening. There would be no stopping tonight.

Chapter Eleven

I woke up naked and sore, my pussy aching and my throat burning. A glass of water and two pills that looked like over-the-counter pain relievers sat on the nightstand...right next to a small bottle of lube. A demand from my stallion with the reason why I should obey spelled out for me. I nearly huffed a laugh—Matthew, again doing whatever he wanted so he could get his way.

Both of us had gotten *our way* for a few hours after lunch, though I could tell he'd held back. He hadn't pushed me as hard as I'd sensed he'd wanted to. He hadn't let go of the leash on his desires. I was okay with his need to control things, though. In fact, I sort of liked it and couldn't wait to experience more of it. What I didn't like was waking up without him next to me.

I rolled over, bringing the sheet with me, my eyes darting almost immediately to the man himself. He sat at the end of the bed, his chest bare and a faded pair of jeans covering his lower body. He didn't say a word, simply watched me with those blue eyes of his. Looking hungry in a way that set my body on fire. Looking slightly lost as well. I had no idea what time it was, where I should be, or if the rest of my stallions might need me for something. All I could focus on was that Matthew obviously did.

"Come," I said, holding up the sheet with one hand and offering my other to him. "I want to feel you next to me."

Matthew stood, his jeans unfastened and hanging low. Showing every dip and curve of muscle from his pecs to his Adonis belt. Looking like some sort of predator on the prowl. I loved knowing I was his prey. Even my fox, who'd been relatively quiet since being with Liam, sat up and took notice of the way Matthew watched us and the sensual way his body moved. Just as intrigued and excited about what was about to happen as me.

"You know, bunny," Matthew drawled, his words slow and languid on his tongue. "If anyone should be giving orders, it's me."

I lay back down, pushing the sheet to my waist and sprawling across his big bed. I brought a hand to my breast, teasing the flesh there. Pinching my nipple as I held his heated gaze. "So give me some. I want you to."

That smirk appeared, the one just this side of wicked. "You might regret that request."

"I could never regret a moment with you, Matthew. Not ever."

He pounced, pinning me to the mattress and assaulting my mouth with his. Rough and strong, his hands grabbed my wrists and yanked them over my head. Holding me in place as he thrust his tongue into my mouth and overwhelmed me with his kiss. I arched into him, craving more. Needing it. Wanting so much to surrender to him and let his personal beast take care of me. Wanting to submit.

And when I finally broke the kiss, I made sure he knew that. "Tell me. Tell me what you want me to do. I'll follow your instructions. I promise."

His answering growl had me shivering, trembling underneath him. But not in fear. Oh no, not even close.

"My bunny wants to play?" He rocked into me, letting me feel how hard he was. Rolling his body over mine. "Because we can do that. I've got all sorts of ideas if you're willing."

"I'm willing." My answer came automatically, my eyes locking on his as I said the words. I had to know what he would do to me, needed to find out how much that domineering personality transferred into the bedroom. If he took over, I didn't have to think, didn't have to decide. I could give him my consent and let him go, let him take me where he wanted to, let him rule my body with his. All of which sounded decadent and exactly like what I needed.

"You might regret letting me do what I want." He moved my wrists to one hand, sliding his other down my arm. I flinched as he tickled across my armpit, moaned as he traversed the swell of my breast and tweaked my nipple. But he didn't stop there. Matthew had plans. He kept moving that hand lower, kept tickling and touching and stroking as he distracted me with his kisses. He slipped his fingers inside, wetting them before continuing on. Kept right on going until he'd slid that evil hand underneath me, until he'd reached the crevice of my ass. Until he had his fingers pressed right up against the only virgin spot left on my body.

"This," he said, growling low and deep. "I want this. Have you ever let someone fuck you here?"

I shook my head, pulling against his grip as he held me down. Excitement and fear mingled in a way that made my breath come faster and my heart pound harder. So hard. He grinned wider.

"Good. I'm going to take you right here, bunny. It'll take some time, though. Gotta get you nice and loose before I shove my cock inside you. Gotta work this little hole a good, long while." He pressed harder, a single, wet digit slipping just inside as I whimpered. "And you're going to love every fucking second of it."

I doubted. I doubted a lot. Matthew seemed to understand that, though. He pulled his hand away and let me go, sitting back on his knees and dragging out his cock to stroke that long, hard beast from root to tip. To tease me with what I knew was to come.

"Are you still willing? Because I'll let you back out if this isn't what you want. Your wholly given consent is what I want more than anything, sweet bunny."

It took me a good minute to let my mind roll through all the possibilities. To give my brain time to catch up to the rest of my body. I could have this—this first experience with Matthew—on my terms. I could give him this gift or not. I could do whatever I wanted, and he'd work with me.

He would give me all the power even as he took control and pushed me outside of my comfort zone.

I loved him for that. "I'm still willing."

Surprise flashed across his face, but only for a second before he was on me once more. Reaching beneath me to grab my ass. To pull my cheeks apart roughly.

"That's my girl. Not so shy, after all, are you?" He kissed me hard and deep, tangling my tongue with his as he brought his legs up to straddle my hips before pulling away. "Flip over, bunny. Daddy's got a lot of work to do before I take my little girl's cherry."

Oh hell... *Daddy*. I'd never thought I'd like that sort of thing, that particular endearment. But when Matthew said it? When he implied he had that position of power over me?

I nearly came. From a single word.

What had I gotten myself into?

Chapter Twelve

Matthew hadn't been kidding about a lot of work to do.

"One more, bunny. Give it to me." He dug his hand into my thigh, his other buried deep inside my pussy. He'd been fucking me with his fingers for what felt like hours, tracking down that elusive G-spot and then torturing it, all in the name of getting me ready for another kind of sex. Of working my body almost to the point of exhaustion. I couldn't count how many orgasms I'd had already, but my body was almost ready to give out on me, my mind shattered by bliss after bliss after bliss.

And he wasn't done yet.

I doubted he ever would be.

"I want to feel that pussy milking my fingers, bunny. One more."

"I can't." I gasped as he released my thigh only to lay a heavy-handed smack across my pussy.

"Can't what?"

I jerked, groaning at the pain of it. Shivering at the pleasure. "Can't, Daddy. I can't come again."

He slapped my pussy again, harder this time. Smacking right over my clit. My body convulsed, every muscle locking down, a scream tearing from my throat as I came and came and came some more.

"That's it. That's what I want. Give Daddy all that pussy juice."

I did. All of it. Every drop. And when I was done, when my body finally relaxed and my pussy stopped clenching his fingers, he placed a kiss right over my clit.

"That's my good girl." The bed dipped as he leaned away, but I was too tired to look. Too proud that I'd pleased him to wonder what sort of sensual torture he had up his sleeves at that point. Or really, non-sleeves, seeing as he was as naked as I was.

When he came back to kneel beside me, he rested one hand on my ass and brought the other around so I could see what he had in his grip.

"What do you think, bunny?"

If he believed I had the energy to think after all he'd done to me, he really overestimated my endurance. "It's sparkly."

Matthew chuckled at my breathy declaration. "It's called a princess plug. It's going to look fabulous in your ass."

I was almost too tired to care. Almost. Okay, I cared. A whole hell of a lot.

"Will it hurt?"

Matthew stopped moving, looking so supportive and sure. "I would never hurt you intentionally. It might make you sore, but you'll get pleasure from that. And if you don't, you tell me, and I'll stop. I promise. Okay?"

I bit my lip and nodded. I trusted Matthew. Trusted him with my body. He, like the rest of my stallions, wanted to bring me pleasure. Pain wouldn't do that, so I had to believe this wouldn't be too bad. And then...

Then, he'd push more than just a plug up there.

"Your cunt is so nice and swollen from all those orgasms. Good and wet for me." Matthew tipped a bottle over my ass, and a cold sensation landed right over my virgin hole. "Still need lube, though. Always lube. I don't want to hurt you, bunny."

He started with a finger—one long, thick digit sliding around my puckered hole and then slipping inside. Thrusting shallow and slow, retreating only to push back in. I fisted the sheets and watched him from an almost upside-down angle. The focus on his face, the solidness. The attention he gave me. That was almost as good as the sensations from where he had his finger inside my body. Almost, but not quite. Because, that finger? It felt good. Really good. Slightly pinchy and a little more pressure than I was used to, but pleasurable enough to make me moan on a deep thrust.

I pushed back, wanting so much, my sore pussy clenching and throbbing with need. "More. Please."

"Oh, you'll get more. I promise you that." He slid up behind me, his cock brushing against my thigh. "You know, it's a good thing I've got you in my bed before Cade and Dalton. They always do everything together." He pressed the tip of his cock into my swollen pussy. Just the tip. Practically teasing me with how shallow he stayed. "And I do mean everything."

Together. As in two at once. As in...*oh my*. But I couldn't think about them, couldn't focus on anything but his finger in my ass and his cock right there, ready to plunge inside me. That fat head sitting at my entrance and teasing me in the meanest way possible. Denying my every attempt to take him inside.

"Matthew, please. I need you."

"And you'll get me, bunny." He removed his finger from my ass, replacing it with what felt like his thumb. Bigger and thicker, it slid inside my lubed hole, making me shake and moan. He worked me that way for a long stretch, in and out, curling that thumb. Smacking my ass for good measure every few beats. And I liked it—I practically sang for more, keening wordlessly as I begged in my head for his cock.

But then he stopped. Froze. Pulled his thumb from my ass and...

Grabbed the sparkly plug.

"Matthew?"

He poured lube over the tapered end of the metal piece, looking so very focused on his task. And when he was ready, when he returned the bottle of lube to the nightstand and brought the plug toward my upturned ass, he smiled. "I love seeing you like this. Head down, ass up, spread wide open for me. You look ready for anything."

I eyed that plug as if it had teeth. "I'm not sure about *anything*."

Matthew stroked his cock once, twice, while staring at my ass before smacking me again. I jerked forward, hissing, pain and titillation mixing together to make me drip with need.

"You trust me?" He met my gaze, one hand holding on to my ass, the other holding that plug.

I couldn't lie to him. "Of course."

"Then be a good little bunny and trust that I want the best for you. The most pleasure. Everything I do is because I know you'll get so much from it." He brought that hand with the plug behind me until I couldn't see it any longer. "Deep breath, and push out at the pressure."

And oh, that pressure. So much, so much. Stretching, pushing, filling me up. I buried my head in the pillow and tried to breathe through it. Tried to find the pleasure in the pain. It wasn't until Matthew dropped a hand and started playing with my clit again, still pushing that blasted plug into my asshole, that I was able to relax just a little.

"That's it. That's my good bunny. Just a little more, then I'll give you everything you want."

Had I been in a different frame of mind, I might have laughed at that. Everything I wanted? He'd given me that hours ago—all the rest we'd been doing had been above and beyond anything I could have even thought to consider possible.

As he pushed on the plug and held on to my ass, I moaned, the stretch lessening, the pressure increasing. He must have made it over the thickest part of the toy. The plug must have been seated all the way. Resting inside me. Sparkly jewel fully on display.

I turned my head, rocking against his hand. Watching him as he stared down at me in what I could only describe as wonder. As deep, lustful need. As something I wanted to see on his face a thousand more times.

"Fuck, that's pretty." He sat back, taking his hand away from my clit to hang on to my hips with both. "I...I was going to go slow, bunny. I swear. But this"—a wave at my upturned ass—"fuck, it's a thing of beauty. I want your pretty pussy wrapped around my cock so fucking bad right now."

My answer came from deep inside me, from some fox mating instinct long buried. From knowing what my man, my mate, my stallion, needed to hear in that moment. "It's yours. Take what you need."

His eyes met mine again, almost shocked yet still arrogant as fuck. "I intend to."

Cock in hand, he teased me. Dragged the head through my slit, wetting it in my arousal before sliding it down to bump my clit over and over. I practically growled, needing him inside me, feeling so damn empty yet full at the same time. But when Matthew thrust forward, when he buried his cock inside me while I had that plug in my ass, I saw stars. Literal stars.

I also suddenly felt completely full, more than ever before. Stuffed at two ends. And I fucking loved it.

"You're so goddamned tight. I knew you would be." He moved like a man possessed, like a man who needed to use my body to come. Who wanted nothing more than to seek his own pleasure. And I was ready to give it to him.

I dropped my head to the mattress, arching my back and letting him slide deeper. The pressure, the dual sensations of his cock and that plug, drove me wild. Left me rocking, groaning, pushing my body back to meet every thrust. Knocked the language right out of my head until the only sounds I could make were wordless ones intending to tell him what I wanted—more, deeper, harder. Everything.

"Fuck, I can feel that plug inside you." Matthew nearly fell over my back, humping hard. Slamming his hips into my ass and thrusting deep. "Makes you tighter. I'm going to come so deep inside you. Going to fill you up until my come drips down those sexy thighs."

Yyyyeeesssss. My orgasm slammed into me, completely stealing my breath with its suddenness and intensity. I screamed, falling forward, my legs shaking uncontrollably as I rode out every blissful second of release. I didn't feel Matthew pull out of my pussy, didn't really take note when he pulled the sparkly plug from my ass either. I definitely didn't notice him moving around behind me. Not until he pressed the head of his cock against my asshole and pushed. Slid inside. One long, slow stroke from tip to root. One single motion that had me crying out, twisting and trying to pull away from the intense pressure. From the feeling of him filling me up in a new way, so much more than his finger or thumb or even that plug. From the way my orgasm wanted to explode into mini ones at the sensations his cock in my ass brought me.

"I've got you, bunny," Matthew said, groaning long and loud as he pulled out slowly and pushed back inside. "Fuck, this ass is so good. So tight. And all mine. I got to take this cherry from you."

He grabbed the headboard above me, fucking harder, thrusting deeper every time. Increasing his speed until his hips were slapping into my ass and I was crying out again. My face pressed into the pillows, my screams tearing from my mouth. Matthew dropped down to cover my back. Grunting with every wild thrust. Slipping his hand between my legs to pinch my clit. That extra sensation, that little bit of pain, did me in. Again. I collapsed as I came, unable to hold myself up. Unable to control a single muscle in my body as pure, sweet, achingly exquisite pleasure took over everything.

Matthew let me fall, pushing my shoulders down with one hand. Pulling his cock out of my ass and coming all over my back. Claiming me. Marking me as his—as *theirs*.

"Property of Hidden E Ranch Stallions" might as well have been tattooed across my back.

"I think I'm going to need a minute," I said when he grabbed at my hips, trying to pull me across the bed. His quiet laugh rumbled through the quickly darkening room, his hands strong and demanding as he moved me where he wanted to.

"I think you're going to need a nap." Matthew kissed my shoulder then rose from the bed, his footsteps retreating across the space. I didn't turn to watch, didn't have the energy to pay attention either. I simply lay on his bed, surrounded by his scent and completely, utterly exhausted.

He came back with a wet cloth, cleaning me up. First my hips and back where he'd come on me, then between my legs, and finally right up the crack of my ass.

"That is so not sexy." My grumble was met with another chuckle.

"Taking care of you in every way is totally sexy. Plus, you're naked—sexy. And my handprints are on your ass—totally sexy. And my come was dripping down your spine—definitely fucking sexy." He leaned down to kiss my shoulder before wrapping me in his arms and pulling us together. "Rest, bunny. You need it."

"Will you stay with me?"

"For as long as I can. I have things to do for the herd once the guys are back, but I'll make sure you're taken care of. You just sleep. I wore your ass out."

Cocky bastard. "You definitely wore my ass out. And my thighs. And my toes."

"Your toes?"

"From the curling. I think they're permanently curled now."

His chuckle turned into a full-blown laugh. "Sleep, silly bunny. When you wake up, we'll get you some food."

The darkness was already taking me when I mumbled something that I thought was "Food sounds good," though by the way Matthew laughed again, I had a feeling that wasn't at all what came out of my mouth. Didn't matter. Nothing mattered but his warm weight against my back, his heavy arm around my hips, and the sleep pulling me into its embrace.

Chapter Thirteen

I woke up in Matthew's bed again, though this time, he wasn't anywhere to be found. What I did find, though, was a glass of orange juice, those same pain-reliever tablets from earlier, and a single wild flower in a little vase sitting right next to a brand-new princess plug. One with a different colored jewel in the end. A promise of things to come from my naughty stallion.

I took my time getting up, giving my body a chance to recover from all we'd done to it. Matthew had definitely worked me over well, and I would pay the price for such a strenuous day. One I'd gladly pay again, just not right away.

A long, hot shower helped, and the pills Matthew had left finally kicking in definitely pushed me halfway back to normal. Ready to face the rest of the herd, I slid one of his button-down shirts over my body, the one he'd strategically left out for me. My men and their claiming.

Though, I liked wearing the clothes of my men, enjoyed their heated glances when I came out wearing one of their shirts hanging halfway down my thighs...and nothing else.

Plus, I found their shirts gave me something tangible of them to focus on when they were away from me. Wearing Matthew's clothes, smelling his scent all around me, offered me more comfort than just about anything else could have at that point. Except Matthew himself.

I headed downstairs, figuring he had to be in the kitchen. All that time spent pleasuring me had probably worked up an appetite in him, and I almost felt guilty that I wasn't there to cook for him. Almost. Because if he'd wanted me to make him or the other stallions dinner, he would have told me to. And I would have obeyed.

But when I reached the back hall, I heard the rumble of multiple voices. The golden light of sunset hung low in the old farmhouse, the shadows deep. Everyone had come home for dinner. Anxiety at what they would all think when I came in smelling of Matthew and wearing his shirt after having been wearing Liam's just that morning hit me, but overriding it was a sense of excitement. My boys were home, and I couldn't wait to see them. To feed them. To take care of them.

I raced into the kitchen, grinning when Tripp greeted me with a loud whistle.

"Look at you, doll," he said, standing up and hurrying my way. "Maybe I should call you 'Legs.'"

I smacked his arm but rose onto the balls of my feet for the kiss he offered. His lips were soft, plush, and yet strong. Perfect for what I needed right then.

"Maybe you should just call me by my name. Maybe all of you should."

That received a resounding chorus of *absolutely not* from all seven of them. Figured.

"Fine, fine," I said, taking in each man in turn. "I smell food. Did someone cook?"

Liam nodded toward the other side of the table. "Matthew took the reins on the evening meal tonight. Figured he owed us, seeing as how we could hear your caterwauling all the way out in the barn this afternoon."

Oh no. My cheeks burned, and I found myself fidgeting with the edge of the shirt I wore. "Sorry about that."

"Don't ever be sorry for enjoying yourself," Liam said, leaning forward in his chair. "We loved hearing you, just made it a little *hard* to get any chores done."

The guys chuckled, and my cheeks grew hotter. Oh boy, they'd been aroused by my yells. That made my mind go skittering off track, and I wondered if they'd each taken care of things for themselves since I'd been…tied up with Matthew. I could just picture Liam with that thick, meaty cock in his hand. Stroking himself off somewhere while he listened to Matthew fuck my ass and make me scream. Liam would look so good doing it, would probably bury his teeth in his lush bottom lip as he tried to hold back his groans when he came. The others…well, I didn't know them enough yet to get a solid picture of what they'd look like, of what they had tucked away in their pants. But my imagination was good. My imagination was damn good.

"Okay, bunny. Quit looking at us as if we're a buffet laid out for your pleasure." Matthew grabbed my hand and pulled me closer, smacking my ass for good measure before tugging me into his lap. "Even if that is sort of the reality of our situation."

As the rest of the guys laughed and started talking over one another, Matthew pulled me in close to whisper in my ear. "You hungry, bunny?"

I nodded and moved to rise from his lap. "I'll just—"

"Quinn." Matthew's commanding voice made the entire table go silent. "Our mate is hungry. How about you make her a plate?"

"On it." Quinn jumped up and headed for the stove.

"Oh no. I can do it."

"Of course you *can*, but we don't want you to. I don't want you to. Today was a lot, more than I normally would have done at one time." Matthew leaned in to kiss me, biting my bottom lip for good measure and moaning when I shivered against him. "You're just too irresistible to stop."

I grinned, turning my attention to Quinn when he set a plate in front of me. "Thank you, Quinn."

"Anytime, sweet girl. You just let me know if you want more."

"Want some tea?" Garrett hopped up and grabbed a glass from the cabinet. "It's sweet."

"Gotta get our sugar fix somehow, ain't that right?" Liam winked at me as my blush returned. Damned traitorous cheeks.

"I'd love some tea. Thank you."

And so my evening went. Matthew wouldn't even let me feed myself —he used his hands to bring small bites to my mouth while Garrett cut the food and organized the plate for him. And when I ran low on the roast chicken he'd made, Quinn jumped up to bring me more. Every one of my men sat there, watching. Talking. Entertaining me as Matthew fed me dinner. And as odd as that would have once seemed to me, at that moment, with those men, everything felt normal. And perfect.

"You look tired, beautiful," Garrett said as he took my empty plate from the table and headed toward the sink. "I know tomorrow's my turn, but I think maybe you need a day of rest to recover from Liam and Matthew."

I wanted to refuse him, but Liam was already nodding before I could say a word.

"That's a good idea. We weren't exactly easy on you." Liam's blue eyes held mine, his concern evident. "You take the day off, sugar. Give yourself time to regain some energy. We'll all be patient with you."

Matthew leaned down to nip my ear. "Not me. I'm impatient. I want in that ass again now."

A shiver raced up my spine, and I nearly moaned right there at the kitchen table. I had a feeling no one would have minded.

"So, it's settled." Liam stood from the table, coming over to give me a soft kiss on the lips before addressing the crowd again. "Waverley gets tomorrow to herself. Matthew, I know you've still got tonight with her—"

"I'll be gentle." He smirked when I spun and stared at him with my eyebrows up. "What? I can do gentle. Sort of." I cocked my head, eyebrows still up, waiting. Finally, he sighed. "Fine. I'm still going to fuck you like the naughty little bunny you are, but I won't do anything too crazy. Maybe we'll even stay in missionary position."

I doubted that. A lot.

Chapter Fourteen

Coffee in the morning with my stallions was quickly becoming my favorite part of the day. Matthew had woken me up at dawn with a full-body massage followed by a hot shower. Together. And though we didn't have sex—he apparently wanted to stick with the whole vacation-day from sex thing—he didn't leave me wanting. Two orgasms for me brought on by his hand and mouth, followed by one for him as he stroked himself off against the curve of my ass.

Might have been the longest shower of my life.

But it had been a great way to start my day, and I'd gotten to see and hug and kiss each stallion before they headed out to do their respective jobs. Even Cade and Dalton—whom Matthew had told me did *everything* together—had each given me a soft kiss to the cheek. My sweet, sexy guys. My stallions. My mates. They were all quickly becoming *mine* in my head, every single one of them. A fact that only brought a smile to my face, a quiver to my tired pussy, and a warmth to my heart.

Their affection and greetings that morning made me feel less uncomfortable about the whole no-sex-day thing, too. Maybe the break wouldn't be a problem, after all. Maybe they really would be patient for their turn to have my full attention. More patient than I would have been.

"What's in your plans for today?" I asked Garrett as I sat down across from him. He and Cade were the last two in the kitchen, Dalton having headed to the basement just minutes before. And after Matthew's comment about them doing everything together, it struck me as odd that they'd separated.

Garrett shot Cade a look. "Guard duty."

"Guarding what?" I took a sip of my coffee, looking at him over the cup. Frowning and setting down my mug when he didn't answer me. "Garrett. What are you—"

"We're guarding you," Cade said, his voice hard and rough. His expression stoic.

I was pretty sure mine had to be a bit more...surprised. "Why am I being guarded?"

Did they not trust me to stay put? Did they think I was going to take off? Hell, was I not allowed to leave? I still had my bus ticket, still had the option to go to Fairview. At least, that's what Liam had promised me. If they were going to keep me some kind of prisoner, then they weren't the men I thought they were. They weren't—

"Whoa, beautiful. Stop." Garrett slid his chair across the floor and grabbed me, pulling me into his lap. "I can see all sorts of pain and anger on that expressive face of yours, so just stop. Tell me what's going through your head."

"You're guarding me, so what... I can't leave?"

Garrett grabbed my arms, looking me square in the eye. "Hell no. We wouldn't force you to stay here if you didn't want to be with us. Cade, tell her."

Cade sat back, all big and confident and one-eyebrow-raised hot. Sarcastic as hell too. "Hell no. We wouldn't force you to stay here."

I nearly laughed even as Garrett sighed in frustration.

"Real good help there, man." He pulled me a little closer. "This isn't about keeping you on the ranch, though we really want you to stay. This is about keeping whatever's chasing you away."

I stiffened, unable to think. Unable to breathe. "How did you know?"

Cade answered that question. "No one runs across the country on a bus, with next to nothing, unless they need to. We've been looking into what made you need to."

"No." I pulled away from Garrett, rising to my feet and pacing the big, open space. "No way. You can't go looking for him. If he finds me, if he comes here, you'll put the entire ranch at risk. I won't have it. I won't let him hurt you."

Cade's lips parted and pulled up, the smile on his face reminding me of a shark ready to bite. "He won't hurt us, woman. I can guarantee you that."

"You don't know him."

"So, tell us," Garrett said, imploring me with those bright blue eyes of his. "Tell us who he is and what he did to you so we can find him. We'll get ahead of him."

But I couldn't. I shook my head, still pacing. An oppressive sensation blanketed me, making me feel trapped and anxious. My fox scratched at my mind from the inside, wanting out, needing to run. To disappear for a bit. Needing me to give her control.

Which sounded pretty damn good at that moment.

"I'm going for a run." I held up my hand when both men rose to their feet. "Alone. I want to be alone."

"No can do," Cade said, already pulling off his boots. "You can run out there all you want, but we're coming with you."

I spun, walking away. Pacing. Needing to find my space but unable to leave them behind. "You guys can't just—"

But when I turned back around, I froze. I wanted to argue, to fight, to demand they let me go, but I had to focus too hard on breathing.

Both men were stripping off their clothes right there in the kitchen.

Boots and socks removed and set aside, collared shirts pulled off over their heads and hung over the backs of the chairs. And when they dropped their jeans—neither wearing anything underneath the thick denim—I had to hold myself up with a hand placed on the counter. Muscles. Muscles upon muscles from shoulder to ankle. Thick thighs and slim waists, rippled abs and broad chests with just enough hair to tease my sensitive nipples when they dragged their bodies against mine. And the rest... I couldn't look away. They were just so damn sexy and hot and *male*.

"I don't want you out of my sight," Cade said, the words almost fuzzy in my head. I couldn't look up at him, couldn't turn my head away from the two cocks jutting straight up in the air before me. Both big and thick, both hard. Garrett's looked to be just a little longer than Cade's, with a curve to it that made my mouth water. But Cade? He was pierced. Motherfucking pierced. The little silver barbell looked like a bow tie for his cock. A thought that almost made me laugh.

"So are we shifting or fucking?" Cade asked, watching me, his hand dropping to grab hold of himself, all stoic disinterest gone from his face. "Because I'm up for either."

"Fucking's off-limits." Garrett stroked his long cock, fingering the head as his gaze burned into me. "You'd better shift, beautiful. You keep looking at us like you're hungry for our cocks, and we're going to find a way to give them to you that won't break Liam's rules."

Yes, please. But my fox howled, still wanting out. Needing to run. And those cocks would be waiting for me. Garrett tomorrow, Cade in a few days. With Dalton. At once.

Yeah, I needed to run.

I shifted right there in the kitchen, the shirt I'd been wearing falling to the floor. I shook out my red fur and strutted closer to my men, bouncing around them in a floaty sort of trot and rubbing against their calves before heading for the door. When Garrett swung open the screen for me, I raced outside, jumping off the porch and running across the driveway toward the woods. Hoofbeats followed, heavy and hard. *Fast.*

Good.

Let them chase me for a while. They might have been bigger, maybe even faster, but I had something they didn't. Agility.

As I ran into the forest, I caught sight of my two mates tracking me from the more open pasture. Big and tall, with black hair covering their muscular bodies and long, flowing manes and tails, they looked regal yet wild. Dangerous, even. They looked like the stallions I knew them to be.

Mine.

There was no way I'd let my past come to take them away from me.

Chapter Fifteen

Two hours running through the fields and woods around the farm refocused my thoughts and left me both reenergized and exhausted. I needed a long bath and a nap if I was going to be of any use for the rest of the day. I raced into the barn, heading for the box of cloaks the men kept handy for moments like this. Moments when someone needed to shift and couldn't just walk around naked. I mean, *I could* walk around sans clothes. I had a feeling my stallions wouldn't mind, but I figured—in the spirit of the no-sex day—I'd better stay covered up.

As I tugged a cloak around my naked shoulders, one of my stallions came trotting into the barn. So big, so heavy with muscle. His black coat shone like a mirror, the muscles rippling underneath it. Something I couldn't resist. I approached with caution, the sheer size of him making anxiety tighten my skin. My heart pounded hard and loud, giving away my fear. My excitement.

But my stallion simply stood, watching me with eyes as cornflower blue as the sky outside. Breathing hard from so much running but refusing to move even an inch. That look in his eye, the careful way he watched me, the way he stood so calm and solid for me—only one man made me feel as safe and cared for.

"Hi, Garrett. May I pet you?"

He tossed his head, snorting once and dropping his neck so I could reach him better. I took that as a yes.

I ran my hand over his face, letting my fingers tickle along his velvety muzzle. Bringing them all the way up to the tips of his ears and squeezing. He closed his eyes and sighed, nudging me for more, that fuzzy top lip of his quivering as I stroked him. Ears to nostrils, around to his heavy cheeks, down under his chin. Every inch. Every dip and curve. Everywhere I could reach.

"You're so pretty." I laughed when he opened his eyes and snorted. Loudly. "Fine. Not pretty. Handsome. You're quite the handsome stallion."

He nodded once before nudging me with his head, greedy for my attention. I loved it, loved that he wanted my touch. That he was willing to stand there and let me rub my hands all over his face.

"You know, I've never ridden a horse."

His head jerked, swinging around to bump his nose against his back. Inviting me up.

"No, not today. I'm a little...sore." I shrugged, blushing at the thought of *why* I had that quiet ache between my legs. Of Liam and his skilled tongue, his thick cock. Of Matthew and his kinky side, his toys, and the way he offered a side of pain with the pleasure he gave. Yeah, way too sore to sit astride such a beast at that moment. "Maybe another day, though. If you wouldn't mind."

Garrett shifted right there, rolling between forms quickly and standing in front of me—human and naked—within seconds.

"Of course I don't mind." He pulled me into his arms, wrapping himself around me and sliding his hands up and down my body. Rubbing my hips, gripping my waist, massaging over my rib cage. "Anything you want or need, we're all here for you. Don't hesitate to ask."

I curled against his chest, loving the warmth of his embrace. The support I found there. That was Garrett—kind and supportive, always watching me to see if I needed something. Always keeping an eye on his herd, too. Attentive...that was how I would describe him. I wondered how that would translate into the bedroom, to how the two of us would come together. Would he be as attentive then, making sure to cater to my needs? Or would that care fall in the face of his own pleasure? Would he take and take and take, using my body for his pleasure before giving me my own?

I almost couldn't wait to find out.

Almost. My pussy was still in recovery mode.

Garrett finally let me go, reaching for a cloak and slipping it around himself before moving to tighten the tie on mine. Covering me fully. Even reaching to tuck my breasts away with gentle hands and a soft smile on his face.

"Beautiful as ever, but I can't concentrate when you're naked. And I need to concentrate right now."

My stomach dropped, and my skin went cold. He wasn't letting me get away from this morning's conversation.

"Garrett, please—"

"What are you running from?"

Yup. Just as I'd thought. All that running, all that petting, all the sweetness—negated with five words.

I turned away from him, folding my arms across my waist, doing my best to hold myself together. "I'm not running anymore, and I'm not talking about this."

Garrett didn't respond, didn't make a noise or a move. He simply waited me out, something I had a feeling was a skill of his. Patience.

I finally turned around and met his stare, not wanting to fight with him. Not wanting to lie either. "Fine. I *was* running. But when Liam found me at the gas station, the worst was over. I had things under control. I'd already gotten away from him."

Garrett's blue eyes turned darker, his lips flattening into a thin line, but he didn't say a word. Still waiting me out. Pushing that patience of his to its limit, it seemed. He might as well have given me truth serum for how well his silence dragged the words from me.

"Garrett—"

"I want a name."

Of course he did. "There's no reason to hunt him down."

"He scared you enough to make you leave your life behind. That's a damn good reason, in my opinion."

Yeah, maybe. But that didn't mean I had to like talking about my past. My mistakes. My stupidity.

"You'll think I'm an idiot," I said, my voice low and quiet.

But Garrett heard me. Heard me and knew just what to say to get me to talk. "I've watched you with my herd, with the others, and I know for a fact that you're being too hard on yourself right now. You're sweet and kind and smart, Waverley. Nothing you're going to tell me about what led up to you running from a threat will change my opinion of you."

Oh. My sweet Garrett. I let him pull me against his chest, let him wrap himself around me. Let him hold me up as he whispered, "Tell me, beautiful. Let me help you."

So I did. "His name's Chance. Chance Evers."

"What kind of shifter is he?"

The weight of that question, the assumptions he'd make once he knew. I almost didn't tell him. But this was Garrett. My sweet stallion with a heart of gold. I could deny him nothing.

No matter how weak it made me look.

But first, I had to get him to let me go. Had to retreat halfway across the aisle. Had to dig deep for the courage to admit my secret.

"He's not a shifter at all," I said, trying hard to keep my voice from failing. "He's human as far as I can tell. But he's dangerous."

Chapter Sixteen

Garrett blinked, the only sign he gave that my admission had affected him. That blink said more than any words could have. Shifters usually didn't mess with humans unless they mated to one. It wasn't a rule; it was just how things were done. We couldn't be ourselves around humans—couldn't admit our dual nature.

But as foxes, we tended to like to be a little sneakier than most other shifters. Sweets and sneaking around—those were our vices. Being with Chance had fulfilled both for a while. Until he'd almost killed me.

"Garrett, please," I begged, not wanting to go into this. Not wanting to bring that bad memory into this place. This ranch. To give it power.

But Garrett would not be swayed. "We need to know, Waverley. To keep you safe. To keep the entire herd safe."

The herd. It wasn't just me anymore. Something I hadn't really taken into consideration. The bitter taste of guilt burned a path up my throat, pulling words from me as I tried not to think about my ex coming to the Hidden E. "He's a pastry chef in Providence, where I'm from. He liked to make me cupcakes."

Garrett grunted. "For your fox's sweet tooth."

"Exactly, though he didn't know about my fox. I kept the secret and played off my obsession as a regular human craving." I shrugged, unabashed about my need for sugar. "It all started well enough—I pretended to be human, he fed me sugary treats, and occasionally we got together for...more than cupcakes."

Garrett growled and cracked his neck, looking ready to charge. To fight. "Is there a reason I would need the details about that aspect of your relationship?" He looked relieved when I shook my head. "Good. You don't need to tell me more, then."

Oh, my poor, jealous mate. I hurried across the aisle, wrapping myself around his body and holding him tight. Reminding him that I was his now. Mate to him and the rest of my stallions. He sighed and yanked me closer, possessing me with his touch, encircling me with his arms and practically pulling me off my feet.

"I'm sorry," I whispered, hating that I had to tell him any of this. It wasn't like he couldn't guess I'd had other partners—sex was sex in our world, beautiful and fun and enjoyable. But usually, once mated, all those past partners got locked away, never to be brought up. Mated pairs could be violently jealous of one another, protective to the death. Having to tell him anything about another sexual partner went against my nature, which was why the herd mating had seemed so impossible at first. This reaction—this anger—was exactly what I'd expected the stallions to feel for each other. It was almost a relief to see it directed at someone outside the herd just to know he cared enough to be angry. Almost.

"Don't apologize for having a life before us," Garrett said, nuzzling my neck. "I could watch any of the other guys here fuck you six ways to Sunday without an ounce of anger or jealousy, but my stallion doesn't like thinking of you with men outside the herd. And neither do I."

"I know." I rubbed my hands over his shoulders and back, my body responding to the nearness of his. But it wasn't the time. I still had a story to tell, one I dreaded. So I did what I needed to, pulling myself from his possessive hold but hanging on to his hands to keep us connected. To keep the memories from sweeping me away. "The first time Chance hit me, I thought I was going to betray my secret and shift right there in front of him."

Garrett looked ready to grab the other stallions and stampede straight to Chance's door. "You should have chewed his fucking hand off."

"Trust me, my fox wanted to. But I figured I should hold it together. I didn't want to have to go into hiding because of some asshole human, you know? So I walked away from him, told him he was never to contact me again. I assumed it was all over."

"But it wasn't."

Not by a long shot. "He started showing up at the cookie store where I worked. It was such—"

"Hang on," Garrett interrupted. "You worked at a *cookie* store?"

I couldn't hold back my grin. "Yeah, at the mall. It was the *best* job."

"Were you paid in cookies?"

"No, but I taste-tested every batch and got to take home what was left over if I worked a closing shift. I *always* worked the closing shifts."

Garrett laughed, shaking his head. "You are *such* a fox."

"Guilty." I shrugged, unable not to. But the lightheartedness quickly disappeared, and I frowned. "I had to quit that job because of Chance. I didn't want him scaring the other workers or the owner. And when he couldn't harass me there anymore, he started showing up at my apartment. One night, I woke up to him *inside* my apartment."

"That motherfucker," he spat, the words harsh and brutal as they exploded from his mouth.

"Yeah. That's about right." I would have called him worse, but motherfucker worked. "By that point, I thought I had tried everything I could think of to get rid of him on my own, so I called for help. I shouldn't have."

"What happened?"

"My neighbor heard me yelling and came over to save me. Chance became a man possessed. I honestly have never seen a human move the way he did. He beat that poor man to the brink of death right there in my living room without breaking a sweat and faster than I could have thought possible. There was something otherworldly about the way he fought, the way he attacked. He's either well trained in some sort of fighting art, or he's not human. I wasn't sticking around to find out which." I shook my head, breathing deeply to settle the sick feeling in my stomach. "He told me no one could save me, that I was next if I didn't do what he wanted. I couldn't risk anyone else getting hurt, so the only option I had left was to run. I know it was stupid not to consider the possibility, but I honestly thought it'd be over."

"He followed you."

My nod was slow, my eyes losing focus as I remembered the fear, the mind-numbing panic every time he appeared somewhere I'd been hiding. When it started to sink in that I might not be able to escape him. "All the way across the country. No matter the city, he'd show up. Pittsburgh, Nashville, Tampa, New Orleans, Dubuque. Everywhere I went, he followed. And everywhere he showed up, he killed someone. Desk clerks, waitresses, truck drivers, hotel cleaning people—all right in front of me as if to make a point. I had no idea how he was tracking me—still don't, not really—but I knew I needed to truly disappear. And to put some serious distance between us."

"So you hopped on a bus to Fairview."

"There's a fox shifter sanctuary there. A ranch where I don't have to hide that side of myself. I thought maybe they could help hide me if I could just get there without Chance knowing. So I gave up every credit card, emptied my bank account, and figured out how to travel across the country without using my identification. And it worked. I haven't seen Chance in months. I was one last ride from Fairview."

"Until you ran into Liam."

Another smile pulled at my face followed by a warm feeling in my chest, like a hug for my heart. "Right. Until Liam."

Garrett sighed, letting go of my hands so he could pace instead. "We need his legal name, his last address, where this guy worked—everything. I want a list of every place you stopped that he killed someone and as many details as you can remember. We're also going to need to take whatever electronics you have with you. Phone, tablet, laptop —anything."

Head—spinning. "Why?"

"He might have put a tracker in them. Don't worry, if Quinn doesn't find anything, you'll get them back. And if this jackass did monitor you with GPS, we'll destroy what we need to and get you something new. Quinn's the tech guy—he'll make sure you've got whatever you want."

"I'm not worried about losing them, but is that possible? Do you think that's how he knew where I was?"

"Possible and likely."

A wave of what felt like ice water flew down my spine as I thought about the cell phone tucked into my backpack. The one that sat turned off and unused. The one that *had* been on when Liam had brought me home with him. "But...then he knows where I am. Chance knows to come to the Hidden E."

"Stop, beautiful." Garrett grabbed my arms, holding me in place. "We already assumed he might be on his way here. That's why we needed you to tell us what you could. Cade and Dalton, they're monsters when it comes to protecting the herd. They've been all over the internet looking up your history to make sure nothing could harm you from your past. And Quinn's been pulling some serious hours himself, searching the web for what we needed to know."

Oh, my silly, overprotective stallions. Assuming my fear was centered on myself. "I'm not worried about me. Well, I am of course, but not wholly. What if he comes after one of *you?*"

"There are seven of us—if he comes for one, he'll get all of us. But most men like that, they don't come for the strong. He won't run head on against any of us guys because together, we're a force to be reckoned with. He sees you as alone and weak, so he'll come for you. But you're not alone anymore, and you sure as hell aren't weak. Especially with your herd backing you up." Garrett hugged me again, kissing the top of my head when I clung to him. When I trembled in his hold. "C'mon, beautiful. I need to get you inside and find Cade so I can fill him in."

"Why Cade?"

"He's the soldier of the herd. The enforcer. He'll take care of the threat."

"You mean like..." I couldn't say it, but Garrett knew.

"I mean make it so this Chance guy never bothers you again."

"You can't just kill him. He's not a shifter—his kind has laws and prisons and things that don't follow our rules." Because in the shifter world, threatening a mate was an offense punishable by death. No other shifter would blame my men for defending me, but humans? Not the same.

"He's violent—you said he killed people."

So many. "Yeah, he did."

"Then he's a direct threat to us, which makes him fair game."

Shifter rules. Again. "But you could end up in trouble with the humans if he goes missing. You can't kill him."

Garrett didn't say a word, just stared down at me. Silent. Not disagreeing but also not promising something he couldn't follow through on.

My men would be going after my human ex.

"Garrett, this is too dangerous. I don't want—"

A growl erupted from my handsome mate, and he picked me up right off my feet to clutch me to his chest. "He abused you, stalked you, murdered people to scare you, and planned to do god knows what to you once he stole you away. He's a direct threat to you, to our mate. For that, his life is forfeit."

If the surety in his eyes, the determination there, was any indication, he meant what he said. My stallions would protect me to their deaths.

A thought that didn't ease the fear quickly burning through my gut.

Chapter Seventeen

Dinner went later than usual that night. Quinn had found a program running in the background on my tablet, the one I used to buy and read books. I'd turned it on every evening while I'd been on the run and even once while at the Hidden E. The way Quinn had glared at the stallions around him when he'd found it told me all I needed to know—Chance knew where I was.

Every one of my stallions sat at the table all through the evening, plotting and planning, setting up guard duty schedules and working to figure out how to keep me safe. All the while, I worried about each of them. My strong, kind Liam with his leader's heart. He would jump into any battle to defend one of his herd, no matter the personal cost. And Matthew, with that wicked grin and filthy mouth. He'd never back down from a fight, even if he thought he couldn't win. Quinn, with those nerdy glasses and his face always buried in some sort of screen—Chance would definitely target him, assuming him the weakest link. I had a feeling he'd be wrong, but I didn't want to find out. Tripp, my funny, playful stallion. The thought of him hurt broke my heart. Dalton and Cade, the two fighters of the group. If one got hurt, would the other be able to keep fighting? Would two fall at once because of their connection?

And of course, my sweet, funny Garrett. The quiet one with the sharp eyes and the quick wit, the one who cheered everyone else up. The supportive stallion with the handsome smile and the heart of gold. Seeing any of the men hurt would break me, but Garrett? I couldn't even imagine the depths of my pain if I lost him. If he ended up hurt because of me.

"So, we're good?" Liam sat back, looking from one man to the next. "Everyone knows their roles and duties over the next few days?"

The guys all nodded, making my heart jump. What had I brought upon them?

"Good. Dalton, Cade, and Garrett—keep sharp tonight." Liam stood, edging his way past Matthew and heading straight for me. "And you, my sweet thing. You should get some rest."

He wrapped his arms around me, holding me close and making me feel safe as only being with one of my stallions could.

Safe and yet sad. And so very foolish. "This is all my fault."

"Aw, fuck no." Matthew took me from Liam, holding me at arm's length. "It's not your fault this human is an abusive, murderous asshole, Waverley. Do you understand? Not your fault. Don't let me hear you saying that shit again."

I nodded slowly, still anxious. Still worrying what would come. But Matthew didn't let me stew—he yanked me into his arms and kissed me, leaning me back and overwhelming every thought process I had until I was a panting, quivering mass of girl flesh. Until the only thing I doubted anymore was if my knees would still hold me up once he let me go and if there was any way possible the other stallions had missed how wet that kiss had gotten me. If they knew what Matthew had done to me.

By the heated looks on all their faces, they knew. They *totally* knew.

"My turn." Quinn took me from Matthew, squeezing me close and kissing my cheek before smiling down at me. "Goodnight, sweet girl. We've got this."

"Good night." I hugged Tripp next—or rather, he hugged me. Actually, he manhandled me, picking me up off the ground and spinning me in a circle. The show-off. Dalton and Cade were next. Each took a cheek, kissing me softly before heading outside for overnight guard duty. At the end of it all, I was left in the kitchen with Garrett.

"Don't get hurt," I whispered, trying hard not to cry.

"Never." He stalked closer, his hands finding my hips and his lips awfully close to mine. "Do you have any idea what time it is?"

What? I looked around but didn't see a clock. "Uh, I don't know."

"I do." He pushed me back, herding me, pinning me between his body and the kitchen island behind me. "It's after midnight."

"Okay. So?"

"The day of no-sex is over."

Oh. Immediately, my pussy began to throb, and my heart beat a little faster. It was his day, his turn with me. He'd been so patient. And me? I was ready for him. Had been all day. I was ready for all my men.

"Shouldn't you be on guard duty?" I asked, even as I slid my hands under his T-shirt and pulled him closer. "I wouldn't want you to get in trouble."

"I am on guard duty, which is why I'm still here." He grunted, pressing his lips to mine just once before pulling away. "Cade and Dalton are outside guards. I'm inside—which means I get you in my bed all night long. No man here would blame me for making sure you were good and exhausted before I tucked you in for the night."

I loved how thoughtful my stallions were. "I do find it hard to sleep lately."

He picked me up, setting me on the edge of the counter and pulling up the hem of the T-shirt I wore. The one I'd stolen from his drawer after my evening shower. He had me naked in seconds, had me leaning back against the hard, stone surface as he sucked and bit my neck before I knew what was happening.

"I'll tire you out, beautiful. Don't you worry about that," Garrett promised before kissing me. And what a kiss—deep and slow, with little lip bites and groans thrown in to drive me wild. He kept my hips pulled tight against his, kept my body on the edge as he kissed me like a man who truly loved kissing. Who saw it as foreplay, an art, a path to seduction. He kissed me like every woman deserved to be kissed. I never wanted it to end.

And it didn't.

Even as he picked me up off the counter and wrapped my legs around his waist. As he stalked through the house, heading for his bedroom. As he carried me inside his room and kicked the door closed. As he pressed me against the wall and fumbled with his jeans.

As he guided his big, thick cock inside my aching pussy.

The kiss kept going. Deeper, hotter, wetter. The man owned my lips even as he thrust into me. As he filled me with his cock. Only then did he stop, did he have to break that kiss to gasp and groan as he started to fuck me.

"Fuck, beautiful. I can't wait. I just can't." He grunted as he thrust deeper, as he pinned me to the wall and took. Not putting me first, not supporting the rest of the herd. Being selfish. I'd wondered if he'd be a bit greedy in the bedroom—now I knew he was.

And it was the hottest thing ever, to see him break.

"Take, Garrett. Take what you need." I bit his lip, digging my nails into the back of his neck as I tried to hold on. But Garrett wasn't a gentleman lover—not soft or sweet in the way he used my body. No, not at all. He pounded into me, fucking me hard. Slamming my body into the wall with every push, every lift, every thrust. I'd never felt a man so deep before, never had such an overwhelming feeling of smallness in comparison to my partner. And while Garrett was big, he wasn't any bigger than Liam. Something about the position, though— the strength of him holding me up, the way his cock invaded my pussy and refused to budge—made him seem even larger. More powerful. More *man*.

"This fucking pussy. So tight. How are you so damn tight, beautiful? Gonna strangle my fucking cock right here." He shook his head, groaning as I clenched around him. As I squeezed and made my pussy even tighter for him. Just to hear more dirty words fall from his mouth. He didn't disappoint.

"Gonna fucking murder this pussy just to bring it back to life. Gonna make you come so hard and long, and then I'm going to eat you right up. Lick every fucking inch of you. Make you come again on my tongue. You're mine for the night, beautiful. I plan to take advantage of every second."

And he did. Rocking into me, dragging his cock out all nice and slow against my tender flesh before forcing his way back inside. He bottomed out inside of me but didn't stop. Didn't even pause. Just kept punching up, intensifying every move. Every sensation. Filling me past the point of pain and back to pleasure.

All the while, he held me against the wall, his forearms bulging and his biceps flexed. So much strength in that move, so much power. The simple act of him holding me up turned me on almost as much as anything else.

Almost, because his cock inside me and his filthy mouth were fucking amazing.

"I can't, I can't." He groaned, pressing deeper, his thrusts losing their rhythm. "Fuck, beautiful. I need...I need... Come for me. I need you to..."

His groan turned pained, his head dropping to my shoulder. He shoved one hand between us, holding me up with the other as he zeroed in on my clit. As he jerked back to look me right in the eye.

"I'm gonna fucking fill you up. Just wait—once you come? Once I feel that hot, little pussy milking my cock? I'm going to come so fucking hard. Fill you right up with my come. Plant my seed and breed that pussy like I know you want me to."

And...I died. My fox practically fell over, clawing at my mind as my orgasm slammed into me. Garrett kept his finger on my clit, pushing hard, bringing so much sensation to the moment. His cock buried inside of me, stretching me wide. His big body pinning me to the wall as those filthy words fell from his normally sweet mouth.

Died.

Dead.

Murdered by fucking too intense to survive.

Garrett snapped his hips harder, groaning through my orgasm as he tried to hang on. Tried to keep going. Tried and failed. When he came, when he finally lost his rhythm, thrusting one last time and holding his cock deep inside me, he practically screamed his pleasure. And he did fill me just as he'd promised. Soaking us both with his come. Making me sloppy wet.

"Good lord, beautiful." He panted against me, circling his hips. Dragging out the tremors and twitches even as his come dripped out of me. "Your pussy was made for me, wasn't it? Hottest thing I've ever felt."

He looked up, smiling that sweet smile again. Looking more like the kind, supportive man I knew him to be than the debauched sex fiend he'd become while in the moment. "I can't wait to taste you—see if that pussy is just as hot on my tongue as it is on my cock."

Okay, maybe not *all* sweet again.

I kissed that filthy mouth of his, sliding my tongue along his as he carried me to the bed. Pulling him down on top of me and wrapping my legs around him to keep him inside of me.

"You need more?" he asked, rocking slowly as if he could go again already. As if he was just as hard as before.

I shook my head but tightened my hold on him, not ready to let him go yet. Not ready to be disconnected. "Just stay with me."

His smile grew, his blue eyes practically shining as they stared into mine. "Always, my beautiful girl. Whenever you need me to stay with you, I'll be there."

And I knew in that moment with a surety that surprised me— Garrett would never break that promise. No matter what.

Chapter Eighteen

Garrett carried me down to breakfast the next morning. Not because he had to but because, at some point in the middle of the night—between coming on his tongue and coming again on his cock—I'd admitted how much it turned me on when he'd held me up against the wall. How knowing he was that strong had made me wetter.

I had a feeling I might never walk on my own two feet around him again.

Not that I'd mind.

The rest of the guys were already in the kitchen, drinking coffee and looking cranky as hell. Liam was the first to spot us. He did his best to give me a smile, but it fell flat. Never reaching his eyes.

"What's wrong?" I pushed out of Garrett's arms, letting him lead me to a chair. Before I could sit, he slid onto the seat and yanked me down to perch on his lap as he held me tight. Supporting me as always. Wrapping his arms around me as well in a protective sort of hold. One that only increased my wariness.

Liam glanced at Quinn, who, for once, didn't have his face buried in his tablet. Instead, the bespectacled stallion stared right at me. And he scowled.

Quinn's expression didn't change as he started talking either. "Chance Evers, also known as Chance Scott, legal name Scott Rivers. Scott did time for assault, domestic battery, and kidnapping a few years back, though not enough. Seems the judge felt a harsher sentence would ruin the poor boy's life, so he got a sweet little sentence of just three months for beating his girlfriend to a pulp, removing a few fingers from her hands, and then refusing to let her leave his apartment until she promised not to try to leave him again. She pressed charges, and Scott went to jail. Once released, the victim mysteriously disappeared, and so did Scott. He reappeared two years later as Chance Scott, claiming to be a chef and landing himself a job at a decent restaurant in New Jersey. Two months after he moved into the area, women started going missing from the neighborhood where he lived."

I took a deep breath, shaky and nauseated. *Missing women.* Likely dead if the way Quinn spoke was any indication. And I'd let that man get close to me. "He killed them?"

Quinn shrugged. "Not sure, but if I had to guess..."

Yeah, he didn't need to finish that statement.

Garrett tightened his hold, practically vibrating with whatever emotion ran through him. "How many?"

"As Chance Scott or Chance Evers? Because his pattern didn't seem to change when his name did." Quinn tossed a folder onto the table, the contents sliding out. Pictures, missing persons reports, all for women I'd never met.

All for women who looked a hell of a lot like me.

"Motherfucker." Matthew used his fingertips to fan out the papers. The *dozens* of papers. So many women, all with dark hair and pale skin, all with heart-shaped faces and plump lips. All with a little extra weight on their curvy bodies. We could have been related.

I couldn't stop staring at them. "They look just like me."

Quinn nodded. "They do, sweet girl."

I swallowed hard, shaking harder. Shivering. "He's not going to stop chasing me, is he?"

"The fuck he's not." Matthew grabbed my arm, pulling me from Garrett's hold. Thankfully, Garrett let me go without a fight. And me? I just wanted my men. Didn't matter to me which one held me so long as someone did because the trembling had gotten worse.

"What are we going to do?" I asked once I had my head buried against Matthew's chest. He grabbed my ass, squeezing hard. Holding on to me as if his life depended on it. But he didn't answer me. No, my dominant one stayed silent, clinging to me. Locking me in place against his body as he let the leader of the group do the talking.

"We're going to get rid of this waste of human DNA before he comes anywhere near you, that's what." Liam looked from one man to the next, staring each down. "Anyone disagree with my plan?"

Lots of head shaking, lots of scowls, and even a heavy "Fuck no" from Matthew. I clung to his shirt, trying to breathe him in. Trying to stop the fear crawling up my spine from embedding her icy fingers in my heart. Trying...and failing.

"He's dangerous," I said, pulling away from Matthew so I could look Liam in the eye. Knowing the rest would fall in line behind whatever he decided. "If you go after him, someone could get killed. Or someone could get in trouble with the humans."

Liam reached over and ran a finger down the side of my face. Looking like a man torn over whether to rage or not. Whether to be soft and quiet and supportive with me or to go full-tilt badass on the world. "If we don't go after him, he'll come for you, sugar. There's no doubt in my mind. And I'd rather be proactive than reactive when it comes to your safety."

His face broke me, made me want to cry. He looked so tortured, so concerned. I couldn't leave him like that. Thankfully, Matthew must have seen the same thing I did because he kissed the top of my head then patted my ass, directing me off his lap and toward Liam. His stallion brethren, his brother-in-arms. *Our* leader.

And that was the moment I knew—there was no way I would ever leave these men. No way I would walk away from my stallions. Before Liam could grab me, before I could be moved from one man to the next, I rose to my feet. Stood on my own as I ignored the questioning looks of the men surrounding the table. It took me a minute to find my purse, took a little longer to dig out the bus ticket Liam had bought me that first day. What didn't take long was ripping it up and tossing the pieces on the table between the seven stallions.

"I won't be needing that anymore," I said, working my way around the table. Running my hand over the shoulders of each man in turn—Cade, Dalton, Tripp, Quinn, Garrett, Matthew—stopping beside Liam. "If you're willing to fight for me, then I'm willing to fight for us."

Liam grabbed me, pulling me into his lap and wrapping me in his strong arms. My back to his chest. Before I could more than sigh, he pulled my legs apart, spreading me to the rest of the room. Exposing me.

"If you're ours, sugar, I think it's time every man got to see what Matthew, Garrett and I already know. How this amazing little pussy is a fucking life-ruiner, and how much they're going to become addicted to making you squirm once they get that first taste."

All of them. Watching. Getting to hear every moan and sigh and... fuck, I was soaking wet at the thought. Knowing they could all see under the shirt I wore, that they could see my bare pussy, turned me on the way nothing else could. One man taking care of my needs was hot—all seven watching was unforgettable. And a lovely distraction from the shitshow I knew was headed our way.

"Use your hands." Garrett winked when I looked up, his lips quirked into that gentle smile I loved so much.

"Fuck hands," Matthew said, sitting deeper in his chair and spreading his legs as he brought his own hand to cover his obvious erection. "Use your mouth. She gets so soft and sweet when you lick her cunt."

I groaned, wanting something...anything. Hand, mouth, cock, I didn't care. Not with all my men watching Liam spread me wide for them. Not with his big body so solid behind me.

"It's Garrett's day," Liam said, leaning down to nuzzle my neck and wrapping his arms tighter around me. "He picked hands."

He slipped a hand between my legs, brushing over my clit with the side of his finger. Teasing me. I arched and groaned, trying to shift my hips. To chase that wandering finger. But Liam didn't let me go. He held me tight, clamping me to him as he bit and sucked on my neck while dragging his fingers around my pussy. Purposely avoiding where I wanted him the most.

"Liam," I whined when he passed right beside my clit for the third time. "Please."

"What do you want, sugar? Tell me."

"Your hand."

He cupped my pussy. "You got it."

Garrett snickered, trying hard to bite it back. I glared at him, widening my knees and tilting my hips out. Garrett had surprised me with his filthy mouth—two could play at that game.

I held Garrett's gaze as I spoke to the man behind me. "I want your thumb on my clit and your big, thick finger in my cunt. No, two fingers. I've been filled with cock for days—a minimum of two will be needed to get me off. And just like when your cock is inside me, I want you deep, and I want you hard. I need you to fuck me with your hand." I shot Garrett a sarcastically sweet smile when his eyes went wide. "Pretty please."

Liam groaned but followed my directions like a good mate, plunging two fingers inside me and pressing his thumb to my clit. "Like this?"

I nodded, gasping as he moved his fingers in and out. As he pressed on my clit and followed my instructions to a T. The wet, sucking sounds coming from my pussy seemed to echo in the kitchen, completely raunchy noises that I normally would have been embarrassed about. But not then, not with my guys looking on as if watching the best porn ever made. Every man had a hand on their cock, some with their pants unfastened, some still over the clothes. Every one had their eyes locked on me, my body, on Liam's hand acting out what I wanted. They were getting off on the show, and I loved every single part of it.

"What else?" Liam asked, breathy and low. "Tell me what you want, sugar."

The roughness of his voice nearly killed me. "Pinch my nipple and rub my clit a little more. I'm so close." I arched back, hanging on to his thighs. Spreading myself so the rest of my mates could see as I whined, "I want to come."

"Fuck, I want that too. I want to feel you squeeze my fingers with this hot little cunt." Liam did as he was told again, tweaking my nipple and making me jolt as he put more pressure on my clit. I shook and shivered in his arms, climbing so close to that edge. Needing one final push to go over.

I got it from Garrett, who grunted and caught my attention. Who must have seen how close I was and wanted to get me to where I needed to be. He knew how, too. Knew exactly what would make me come.

His filthy, filthy mouth, which he used as he stroked that long, thick cock of his.

"Feel good, Waverley? You like his fat, rough fingers buried deep inside your pussy? I wonder if he can feel my come from this morning. Wonder if he knows how much you like it when I tell you I want to fill you up and make you sloppy. How much you want to be bred."

That did it. I came with a yelp, gripping Liam's arms and arching back against him. He pulled me through every quake and quiver, slowing down but not removing his hand from between my legs. Rubbing and petting and teasing me right to the end of my orgasm. Until I collapsed against him in a puddle of flesh without bones.

He chuckled when I finally stopped mumbling nonsense. "Well, that was something to see, I'd imagine."

"Fuck right, it was." Matthew grabbed a napkin, wiping off the evidence of his own orgasm from his jeans. "I think I need another shower."

The other guys seemed to agree, some looking sated, others on edge. I had a feeling we'd be out of hot water within fifteen minutes.

And Garrett? Well, he seemed ready to grab me from Liam and take me back to his room, which actually sounded like the perfect plan.

I leaned back, kissing Liam softly before whispering, "Thank you."

"Anything for you, sugar." He patted my ass as I rose to my feet, a move reminiscent of Matthew. I passed my second lover, reaching down to run my fingers over his collar. Keeping my eyes on Garrett's. All the way around the table I went until I stood in front of my sweet, filthy mate. The one assigned to guard me personally. The one I owed my time and attention to.

I reached for his hand. "Coming?"

He smirked, jumping to his feet and picking me up almost in one move. He was already headed for his room when he answered me.

"Every fucking chance I get."

Chapter Nineteen

Garrett woke me up the next morning with sweet kisses to my cheek, a cup of coffee in one hand, and his other grabbing my ass nice and hard.

"Morning, beautiful."

I grumbled a good morning, too tired from a full day and night of him fucking me every which way to be willing to smile just yet. He'd gotten more than his twenty-four hours with me because of how he'd started right at midnight, which was fine by me. But my body was feeling those extra hours like whoa.

He laughed at my crankiness, setting the coffee on the nightstand and curling up behind me. "You ready for Quinn today?"

That got my attention. "I don't know. Am I?"

Garrett stayed quiet for a long moment before nuzzling my neck. "I think so. He's not as kinky as Matthew and not as…mouthy as me. If you're into voyeurism, he might be just your speed."

Well, damn. "He likes to be watched?"

"He likes to do the watching."

"So yesterday morning…"

"Yesterday morning was probably a wet dream come true for him."

Garrett groaned, grinding his hard cock against my ass. "It wasn't too bad for the rest of us either."

I giggled and patted his hip. "You've been inside me for like thirty hours. Save it for next time, big boy."

"But it might be a while before you come running back to my bed." He rolled me over, smiling down at me, looking almost carefree. Almost. "Quinn wouldn't mind so long as he got to watch."

He waggled his eyebrows comically, making me laugh again. A fun moment in the middle of what felt like looming chaos. Which had to be his intention. Distraction.

"Thanks," I said, tucking his wavy hair behind his ears. He grinned and kissed me, patting my hip as he rose to his knees.

"C'mon, my beautiful Waverley. The day awaits your presence, as do the rest of your mates."

I gripped his arms, hanging on. Suddenly nervous. "Are you on guard duty today?"

He blinked, not smiling. Not joking. "Yes. We all are."

I hated that, hated knowing they'd be putting themselves in danger. That my past was interrupting their business, their lives, our future. I hated everything except being with them.

"You be careful, okay?" I whispered, fighting back tears that only would have made the situation harder. "Don't take any risks with Chance. He's human, but he can hurt you. He can hurt any one of you."

My stallions. My mates.

Garrett leaned down, brushing his lips against mine. "I'll be careful. I promise, beautiful. As will the rest of the guys."

There was nothing else I could ask of him.

I showered alone, thinking about my men. Worried about them. They had to have all made it through the night just fine if Garrett was in such a good mood. A comforting thought. And I'd do my best to keep an eye on them. To protect them from Chance and all his fuckery. Because at the end of the day, the stallions of the Hidden E Ranch were mine to love and care for. My men, my family, my future.

And nothing would ever come between me and my mates.

Chapter Twenty

My day with Quinn started with me being chased down the hallway by Garrett and Tripp. The two had me giggling and breathless by the time I reached the kitchen. Most of the rest of my stallions sat around the table, drinking coffee and eating a breakfast I hadn't made for them.

"You know, if you keep letting someone else do my job, I'm going to feel irrelevant." I smiled and leaned down to kiss a very tired-looking Liam, sighing when he grabbed me by the hips and pulled me closer. He buried his face in my breasts and held me tightly, clinging to me as if afraid to let me go. I understood that fear, felt the same thing. I ran my fingers through his hair and down his neck, trying to give him as much comfort as I could. Trying to help him while soothing my own soul.

He held me long enough for the other guys to head outside for work. Each man stopped to give me a one-armed hug or a kiss to the cheek before walking to the door and disappearing into their day. Everyone but Matthew, who pinched my ass hard and ran a hand over Liam's head before leaving us alone in the kitchen. All had looked concerned, all had seemed anxious. That wasn't good news.

But when Liam finally sighed and pulled away from me, he smiled. "Sorry about that, sugar. It's been a long night."

Because of my ex. "Any updates on where Chance might be?"

Liam patted my thigh and tugged me into his lap, feeding me bacon as he shook his head. "Not yet. We tracked him all the way across the country, but Chance sort of disappeared when he got to Arizona."

"So, he's here?"

"Maybe, maybe not. Either way, we've got you. You *will* be safe with us."

I shook my head at my silly stallion. "I'm not as worried about myself as I am about all of you. He might hurt you."

"We're all more worried about you." Liam brushed my hair back and nuzzled my neck before tapping me on the hip. "Quinn's been locked upstairs for days staring at computer screens and doing all the digital legwork. Why don't you head on up there and give him a good distraction?"

I nodded, still snuggling him, too worried not to want to cling to each and every one of my mates. Liam chuckled and stood, taking me with him. Forcing me to stand on my own. Pushing me toward the stairs leading to the attic room where Quinn lived.

"Go on. He'll be your guard for the day, so the two of you can get to know one another. And don't worry—he won't spank that delicious ass of yours for being so late." Liam shot me a wink. "Unless you want him to, of course."

I chuckled and headed for the stairs, ready to get to know the quietest stallion on the ranch. I climbed slowly, anxiousness heavy in my chest and fluttering in my gut. Stallion number four. The computer guy. The one who usually had his face buried in a tablet or a phone. The one Garrett had said liked to watch.

And yet, with all that, the only thing I could think about in regard to Quinn was those glasses. I had a thing for them—a bit of a kink, perhaps. A naughty professor fantasy. Whatever, those dark frames sitting in front of his blue eyes were hot.

Darkness cloaked the attic room, leaving shadows in all the corners and a sense of gloom to the place. Some sort of funky metal music played softly, leading me toward the far end. Toward where I could see lights dancing on the ceiling for some reason.

"You're welcome up here, sweet girl. C'mon over." Quinn's voice carried across the room, calming a little of my nervousness. I followed it around a corner, knowing exactly why those lights had danced on the ceiling when I finally saw where he sat.

Screens. Twelve of them, all as big as televisions, all mounted to the wall ahead of me. All showing different things, most of which I couldn't figure out. And Quinn—he sat in what looked like a big, dark beanbag chair, a keyboard in his lap and those sexy-as-fuck glasses perched on the bridge of his nose. What was it with me and those glasses?

Of course, he was handsome—all my stallions were. It was like some sort of genetic lottery. Horse shifters were apparently all ridiculously hot. Or at least, mine were. But only Quinn wore glasses, and something about them spoke to me. Made me want to see them askew as I rode him. Made me wonder if he was like Clark Kent and Superman.

Hopefully, I'd find out. "I understand you're my guard for the day."

"Yep. Just you and me, all alone in this big old attic all day. Whatever will we do with ourselves?"

I knew what I wanted to do. Quinn must have known where my mind would go with that comment, because he sat a little deeper and grinned. Letting his knees fall open. Letting me get a good, long look at him.

He didn't wear a shirt, just a pair of baggy gray sweatpants that did nothing to hide the bulge he sported. The muscles of his chest were thick and well defined, leading to abs that were made for licking. And those glasses.

Those glasses would be the death of me. I'm pretty sure I whimpered when he pushed them up his nose.

Quinn reached for me, holding out his hand. "C'mere, pretty. Come stand over here."

I stepped a little closer, trying to keep my nerves and excitement at bay. Failing, but trying. Quinn tugged me around the front of the beanbag and looked me up and down, almost inspecting me. Which was fine—I might have been doing the same thing.

"I'd like to see your fox, if you wouldn't mind," Quinn said, leaning back, staring at me with an almost excited sort of interest.

That request threw me for a loop.

"My...fox?" The others hadn't asked to see her. Some had gotten a look, of course—my guards while I'd taken my runs through the woods. But no one had specifically *asked*.

Quinn shrugged. "I'm a visual learner, and I've never seen a fox shifter up close. You don't have to if you don't want—I don't mean to make you uncomfortable."

I remembered Garrett's words, about how Quinn liked to watch. Which was probably a little off. The computers, the tablets, the screens before him, the way he seemed to inspect me as he looked me over, wanting to get to know my fox... Quinn didn't just like to watch, he liked to *see*. To have whatever he was studying right before him so he could visualize the details instead of reading about them. I could understand that.

I could also give him the education he wanted.

I stripped off the too-large T-shirt I wore—the one I'd "borrowed" from Garrett—yanking it over my head and dropping it to the floor. My panties went next with me bending over to drag them down my legs so I could step out of them. Quinn said nothing as I undressed, just sat there and watched me from behind those black glasses. A small smile playing on his handsome face and his eyes locked about a foot below my face. Breast man—got it.

"You ready?" I asked, cocking a hip and giving him a wicked grin that Matthew would have been proud of.

Quinn tore his eyes away from my breasts. "You're getting more comfortable with us. You weren't this brazen with Liam."

No, I wasn't. "I didn't know him then."

Quinn hummed, taking another good, long look at my breasts. "You know us now, though."

"Yes," I whispered. "I'm comfortable now. I've chosen to stay with my mates—that means all of them. No point in being shy."

Quinn smiled all slow and wide, bringing his eyes to meet mine again. "I've seen the way your pussy clenches when you come on another man's fingers. No need to be shy whatsoever."

Yeah, that little show would not be forgotten anytime soon. By me or my mates. And if the way Quinn was staring at my pussy was any indication, he might want to relive the moment. Maybe participate this time.

I'd like that too.

"So," I said, taking a slow, seductive step closer to him. "Do you want me to shift still?"

He seemed to shake himself out of whatever he'd been thinking. "Yeah. Please do, sweet girl. I've been dying to get an up close and personal look at you."

In my fox form. We'd probably get up close and personal as humans —naked humans—later. I was okay with that, so I did what he asked. I shifted right there in Quinn's attic, standing in front of his wall of screens. My inner fox stretched as she appeared, working out the kinks and knots in her muscles. Wanting to run to get her blood pumping. But she didn't run—instead, she inched closer to Quinn. We both wanted to be near our mate, it seemed.

"Pretty." Quinn leaned forward, petting me. Running his hand over my coat and making me want to purr like a damn cat. "Your fur is amazingly soft. I hadn't expected that. And this color—the oranges and reds have a depth you can't see from farther away. You really are a beauty."

I hopped into his lap, forcing him to sit back, rubbing myself against his bare chest so he could feel just how soft my fur was. So he could get a real good look at my colors.

Quinn dragged his hand down my spine, even running his fingers over my tail all the way to the tip. "This tail is fucking sexy, sweet girl. I bet Matthew already used a plug on your ass, didn't he? Yeah, probably something sparkly for you. I'd buy you one with a tail on it. See if you'd like to be my little fox even in human form." He ran his hand over me again, making me mewl in delight. "Fuck, that sound is like a mating call to my stallion. Shift back for me. I need you human for this."

I shifted, falling into his lap when I did. Naked and shaky and feeling so much lust for the man who kept his hands on me. Who kept petting me, even when the soft fur was gone.

"There you are," he said, tucking my hair behind my ear before turning me around. I laid back against his chest, spread my legs over his, and simply enjoyed being with him for a minute. Enjoyed learning the feel of him, the idiosyncrasies that made him Quinn. The warmth of his body against mine.

Quinn kissed my neck, wrapping his arms around me so he could reach his keyboard. As he typed, the kisses turned to little nips, something that had me moaning and writhing in his lap. Something he chuckled about.

"You needy already, sweet girl?"

Yes. Always. How could I not be with so many handsome men around me all the time? Quinn didn't seem to expect an answer, though.

"Okay, time to do a bit of work before we get to the fun." He typed for a little while, making the screens change even as he bit down close to my collarbone. Multitasking like a boss. "See that screen? The one in the middle. I want you to take a good look."

I tried to focus, but Quinn had stopped typing and had brought his hands back to my body. To my breasts, to be precise. He tweaked and kneaded, following me as I arched into his touch. Bringing his head down to suckle softly on my shoulder—to tease me with what that mouth could be doing to my nipples—before popping off.

"Look, sweet girl. Just for a minute. I need to know if I'm right."

My body didn't want me to look. It wanted me to feel, to fall into the lusty haze of being touched by Quinn. Still, I looked. Wanting to do what he said. To please him even if only by acknowledging what he wanted. I looked...

And then I nearly screamed.

My ex, Chance, whose real name was apparently Scott, seemed to be staring right at me.

Chapter Twenty-One

A chill shot down my spine. "That's him. That's Chance."

"I figured as much. He's quite the bastard. The stuff I've dug up on him..." Quinn shook his head and released a heavy breath. "It's fucked with my head. To think that could have been you—victimized and tortured and taken away forever."

When he shuddered, I pressed back, angling myself so I could place a kiss on his chin. "But it wasn't. I got away. I made it here."

"Yeah, you did. You got to us. You made it to Liam, and he brought you home." He slid a hand between my legs, holding me tight while teasing me at the same time. "Speaking of Liam, do you know how hot your little show with him made me?"

I shivered as he ran a knuckle over my clit, gasped as he flicked me right at my opening. "No. How hot?"

He cupped my pussy, fingers slipping inside and heel of his hand pressing deliciously against where I was so sensitive. "I jacked off six times thinking about it, and I'm still so fucking hard. Seeing my mate being pleasured so thoroughly by a stallion in my herd? I didn't think there was anything hotter."

He thrust his fingers deeper, three at once, gripping me from the inside and pulling. Squeezing in a way I'd never experienced. Making me writhe and mumble, trying to call for him. Trying to beg him for more.

Quinn chuckled, the sound much darker and more deviant than I'd thought would come from him. "*This* is going to be hotter. Having you ride my cock will be more intense than watching you. And I love to watch."

I trembled as he moved his hand inside me, against me. All over me. Palm on my clit, fingers deep, he held on to my pubic bone and squeezed his hand closed, shaking me. Making me want to come faster than I'd ever experienced. The sensations, the pressure, were totally new. Totally wrong and yet so damn right. I could barely breathe, couldn't speak. I wanted more of what he gave me, wanted to experience what an orgasm from that squeezing-shaking motion would be like. Wanted to know why it felt so good. Why it made me so damn wet.

Quinn grunted as he thrust upward, hips and hand working against me. Pressing that thick cock to my soft ass. So firm, so stiff. Every inch of him so hard, and I couldn't wait for him to fill me. For him to come inside me. But he didn't make a move to use his cock. He kept his hand busy, though. Kept the other one on my thigh, pulling my legs open. Holding me in place.

At least, until he didn't.

Letting go of my leg, still keeping the fingers of his other hand fucking my pussy, he reached for his keyboard and clicked a few keys. The picture of Chance disappeared.

"I'm going to hunt that fucker down for you," Quinn said, clicking more keys in a slow, stuttered pattern. Still multitasking, yet not as well as before. "I'm going to make sure our girl is safe."

A few more keystrokes and every screen changed. It took me a moment to understand what I was seeing, but once I did...

"Oh, fuck. Quinn." I grabbed his hand, the one between my legs, and pushed. Wanting him deeper, needing more. There, on every single screen, was us—live video from multiple angles of the two of us in that exact moment. Four. Four angles. There must have been cameras all over his room, recording everything, which was so...hot and weird and tantalizing all at the same time.

And yet, it made sense. All of my stallions had been unique so far, had taught me what they liked. What got them off. This was no different. Garrett had said Quinn liked to watch. It was my job to give him a show.

I angled myself a little more, making sure the camera in front of us got a good shot of what he was doing to me. Made sure to spread my legs a little wider so he wouldn't miss a single second. Quinn didn't say anything, just kept moving his hand. Kept rocking his hips so his cock rubbed against me. Kept watching me on the screen and in his lap. Fantasy and reality. Watching and participating.

I waited until I caught his eyes on the screen, until I knew he was watching the full-frontal view of me, before I reached up to grab my breast. Fingers and thumb tweaking my nipple, I lifted and moaned, circled my hips harder, and clenched my pussy around his fingers. He grunted, his hips jerking at the same time as if unable to hold back, his hands gripping me so tight. Shaking the one between my legs in a way that made me want to scream. So good. So close. So, so close.

"Look at you, sweet girl," he whispered into my ear, still watching my hands as I worked my breasts. "Look at what a little tease you are. I put the cameras on because I wanted you to see yourself come, but you're taking over the show, aren't you? Is this you trying to make me want you more? Trying to get me to the tipping point so I make you come, and then you'll let me fuck that greedy pussy?"

I nodded, sliding down his body a bit, wanting so badly for that hand to be the hard cock against my back. Wanting to ride my stallion and see *him* come on the screens before us.

"Tell me, Waverley." Quinn flicked my nipple, sending a bright shock of pain straight to my clit. "Tell me you want me to fuck you."

"I do. I want you to fuck me. Fuck my greedy pussy, Quinn."

He yanked his hand from my pussy, leaving me empty for too many seconds as he tugged his sweatpants over his hips and lined us up. As he ran the head of his cock through my slit before pressing inside. Slowly. Too damn slow.

"I still want you to see yourself come, sweet girl. It's so damn beautiful the way you surrender to your pleasure. How you embrace that side of yourself." Quinn lay back, holding my hips so I couldn't slide down on him. Adjusting his position so he could see the screens before us. "There we go. You want my cock, you can have it. Take it, sweet girl. Ride me hard and take what you need from me. Let me watch you get yourself off on my cock."

Hearing those words, seeing them come from the mouth on the screen, from the dirty professor with the crooked glasses and the wild hair who peered back at me, was about as hot as anything I'd ever experienced. Without waiting for more, I sat back and down, forcing his cock deep inside me in one go. Quinn jumped and groaned, gripping my hips as I began to move. Holding on hard enough to leave fingerprint-shaped bruises, I was sure. I couldn't wait to see them—to be marked by him. To have the evidence of his loss of control on my body.

But first, I needed to watch him come.

I started with hip rolls, letting his cock slide in and out of me with the gentle motion. That was good—Quinn groaned and grabbed me, biting his lip as he watched my body move over his. But it wasn't enough. I wanted him to break, to come completely undone, so I shifted my legs until my feet were planted on the ground, and I bounced. Up and down, harder and faster. Never letting his cock slide out of me but coming close every time. And the cameras—they caught every second. Showed exactly how shiny his cock was from being inside my pussy, how hard and pink it looked. Showed how my pussy swallowed that thick piece of flesh on every downstroke.

Quinn cursed and thrust up into me, his eyes mostly locked on the screen before us. The one that had the best angle of his cock sliding inside me. I watched too. Both of us groaning and moving and rutting against one another as we watched his cock moving in and out of my pussy. It was so surreal—to see it and feel it at the same time. So addictive. And when he reached for the keyboard and hit a few buttons? When the camera zoomed in close enough to see my pussy juice dripping down that thick, hard cock? Indescribable. I almost came just from that image.

Almost...

It was on a hard thrust from Quinn that his glasses slipped. Something so simple hit me right in the gut, sending tingles through my pussy and throwing me over the edge of desire. The crooked frames made him look debauched, well-fucked, and wild. Exactly what I wanted him to be, and I couldn't resist for another second. I came, squeezing his cock as my hips jerked. As my pussy swallowed him whole and wouldn't let him go. As I chanted his name and dug my fingers deep into the muscles of his thighs.

Quinn groaned and grabbed me by the stomach, pulling me back against him as he came with me. As he shot his come inside me. As he held me in place and bit my neck before groaning against my ear.

"See what I mean? So fucking beautiful when you come."

And I had to admit, I agreed with him. Our pleasure was a gorgeous, enticing thing. Something I couldn't wait to watch again.

Which reminded me... "Did that record somewhere? Can I get a DVD or something?"

Quinn laughed and pulled me closer, not making a move to pull out just yet. "Come on up here anytime, and we can watch it together. Hell, we can make a hundred videos like that and put them on loop."

Because he liked to watch. Apparently, so did I.

I leaned back and kissed his soft lips, cupping his chin. "Sounds perfect."

Chapter Twenty-Two

"I want to show you something, sweet girl."

I groaned from my spot sprawled on the floor in front of the beanbag. Quinn had kept his promise—he'd fucked me a few times already, filming every one. Some we watched as we were in the moment; some we didn't. Those would be fun for later. To see me riding him again, facing him as he sucked on my nipples. To watch his expression change as I took him deep into my throat and groaned around him. To witness the way he lost complete control and slammed into me as he had me on my knees before him. All would be a treat to watch.

Just not yet—I'd never been so exhausted by sex.

"If you want to show me one of our sex tapes, I'm going to have to say not right now. I'm too tired for another round."

Quinn's body covered mine, his hand running up my thigh as he leaned over and licked my neck. "Did I wear out this perfect little pussy?"

I shivered, unable not to respond to him. "Yes. You wore me out completely. Though, if you want more of me riding your face, I might be able to be talked into it."

His laugh warmed my heart, and his hands lifting me up to put me in his lap brought more comfort than I'd ever thought possible. Sex with

Quinn was wild and crazy, but it was fun too. Easy. And he was a snuggler. That was an amazing bonus. I liked being wrapped in his arms or lying across his chest. Liked the physical connection. And he obviously did as well, because he took advantage of every opportunity to touch me, to feel my weight on him, to be flesh-to-flesh. Maybe all that time in front of screens had left him a bit disconnected, because now that he had me with him, he couldn't stop touching me.

A fact that didn't bother me in the least.

"Here," Quinn said, shifting me on his lap and reaching for the keyboard again. Just like the first time. "Look at this with me."

One screen changed to a video, an overhead view of the farm. It zoomed in as I watched, focusing on the driveway between the house and the barn. Suddenly, a person appeared in the bottom of the frame, coming from the house and heading toward the big doors of the barn. No, not just a person. Me.

"You went outside yesterday all by yourself."

Such a normal, everyday thing to do. It actually took me a second to remember. "I'd wanted to shift and run for a few minutes. My fox gets antsy when we're stuck inside too long."

"I know, sweet girl. But until we catch this Scott-Chance fucker, I don't want to see this again. If you go out, one of us goes with you. No matter what."

"Quinn, that's—"

"Excessive?" He brought his lips to my ear, dropping his hands to my thighs to hold on to me with a grip just this side of painful. "Do you have any idea what it would do to us to see you hurt? It would kill us. We'll give you as much privacy and alone time as we can, but we can't let anything happen to you. We want you safe with us—we've waited so long for you, little fox."

I had no argument for that. No fight. They wanted me safe, and I wanted the same thing for them. For all of us to be secure and happy and mated together, without some threat from my past. I didn't like being controlled, but I couldn't intentionally do anything to upset my guys. So I nodded, and I snuggled closer to him. And I breathed him in as he finally turned off all the monitors.

"If that's settled, I think we should head downstairs," he said. "It's lunchtime, and my mate needs nourishment."

"Pretty sure you nourished me not too long ago."

He chuckled, his chest rumbling. "Did you just make a dick-sucking joke?"

"Technically, I made a swallowing-come joke. But similar."

"Fuck, I love you." He placed a big, wet, sloppy kiss on my shoulder. "C'mon, sweet girl. Let me feed you something other than my cock this time."

We made it to the kitchen just as Matthew and Tripp came in from outside. Both shirtless and sweaty, with rumpled hair and reddened cheeks. Delicious.

"You missed a hell of a game of one-on-one football, bunny." Matthew grabbed me away from Quinn, pulling me against his sweaty, muscled chest and bending me backward so he could kiss me deep. I loved the feel of his tongue in my mouth, loved the idea of watching him and Tripp play football—preferably naked—even more.

"Next time, I want to watch," I whispered when he finally released my mouth.

"Sounds like Quinn's rubbing off on you."

My smile was unstoppable. "Maybe so."

Matthew's blue eyes sparkled, the little deviant in him close enough to the surface to call to my own. "Hmmm. That could be a fun kink to play with the next time you're in my bed."

Before I could answer him, Tripp yanked me away and tucked me against his big, beefy body. "I get her next, jackass."

"Yes, but I have her now." Quinn tugged on my arm, staring down Tripp until he finally released me. There was no anger, though. No jealousy. This was just good-natured fighting over the one toy they all wanted to play with. Me. And I liked every single second of it.

"Let me feed you boys." I headed for the refrigerator. "Sandwiches okay? I can make them with the leftover fried chicken from the other night."

Tripp groaned, sounding almost pained. "Damn, that sounds good. And I get to watch your ass shake while you make them. Win-win, doll."

I shot him a smile over my shoulder and got to work. As the boys talked about their perimeter walks, the camera system they were upgrading, and planned out how they'd handle the overnight duties coming up, I made them lunch. Making sure to swing my ass and hum just for Tripp. He seemed to enjoy the show, groaning and clapping whenever I got a little more into the moves. Matthew just shook his head while Quinn sat back with a satisfied smirk on his face. Three of my boys, together. I loved it.

Sandwiches made and sides of coleslaw and potato salad in pretty serving dishes, I headed back to the table to serve them.

"Where's yours?" Quinn asked, frowning down at his own plate when I didn't set one in front of my seat next to him. "You have to eat lunch too."

"I'm grabbing it right now." I headed back to the refrigerator and pulled out the pastry box Matthew had gotten me, grabbing the last two treats from inside. I grinned as I made my way back to the table, unable to hold back my excitement over my lunch.

"Pastries?" Tripp looked adorably confused. "You only want sugar for lunch?"

"Yes." I took a bite, moaning, licking the crumbs of sweet, soft goodness off my fork as the guys all watched.

Tripp finally shook his head. "Well fuck, doll. If you're going to make sounds like that, I'll feed you junk food all day."

"And I would thank you for it. With every inch of my body." I shot him a wink before going back to my lunch. So sweet, so delicious. So perfect. After a day of heavy activity, I needed the sugar rush.

Quinn leaned closer, grabbing my hand so I couldn't bring another forkful to my mouth. "Can I have a taste?"

I nodded, trying to move my hand, but he held me still and leaned a little closer. I licked my lips and smiled, knowing what he wanted. Ready for it. He kissed me deeply, slipping his tongue inside to tangle with mine. Stroking in a way that was a promise for things to come.

"Sweet," he said when he finally pulled away and licked his lips. "Not as sweet as you riding my face, but sweet all the same."

Something warm and right exploded within me, something that had my eyes tearing up and a smile brightening my face. Quinn tilted his head, watching me with curiosity.

"What are you thinking, sweet girl?"

I shrugged, glancing at Matthew then Tripp, my smile broadening. "I'm happy. I...there's nothing else. I'm just really happy here."

All three men grinned, and Quinn pulled me into a hug and kissed the top of my head.

"Good. But we're not done with you yet. Not by a long shot."

"Not ever," Matthew added, raising his glass of sweet tea in my direction.

"Yeah. You're stuck with us now, doll. Better get used to it." Tripp laughed, shooting me a wink before diving back into his food. The room dissolved into conversation and laughter, all four of us enjoying a meal together. And as the others joined us—as the group around the table expanded to include all seven of my stallions and I had to move to sit on Quinn's lap to give them each a place to sit and eat—the happiness within me grew.

This was a dream life. One I refused to give up. Chance could come for me, but I wouldn't be afraid. I would fight to the death to protect what I'd found.

Chapter Twenty-Three

Quinn and I spent the rest of the day holed up in his attic room, playing video games and basically hiding from the world. I'd been right about him—he was a snuggler. A cuddly, needy, tactile sort of person. If we were sitting beside each other, he would tangle our legs together. If I had to leave him for something—bathroom breaks, running downstairs to grab snacks or drinks—when I came back, he would immediately pull me into his lap as if he needed to reconnect. I liked it. A lot.

What I didn't like was him falling asleep practically on top of me. I could hardly move under his weight, and breathing had become more difficult than I cared to let it be. But my lovely Quinn slept so peacefully, I hated to disturb him. Still, I needed up.

It took me several long minutes to untangle myself from his hold, to slide myself out from under his heavy body. It didn't help that he kept reaching for me, tugging me closer even in his sleep.

Eventually, I escaped his hold and rose to my feet, staring down at him. Pink cheeks, messy hair, eyes closed in sleep. Still so handsome, even without the glasses.

"You should have been an octopus shifter, not a stallion."

Quinn slept on, so I headed for the stairs and the kitchen. I needed sweet tea and a cookie or two. Something to give me a little boost since I had a feeling it would be a late night with my nerdy professor. In fact, I had a feeling that was his job—to keep me occupied while my other stallions were off doing other things. Dangerous things. I hated that but was quickly coming to accept their concern and willingness to fight for me. I'd fight for them, too.

I was eyeing the contents of the refrigerator—wondering if I could get away with baking a cake just for me—when the back door opened. Tripp came storming inside, his eyes hard and his expression fierce. Ready for a fight. I stumbled back a step, almost afraid. The Tripp I knew was a jokester, the playful, sporty one. Not this...animal.

Tripp froze, staring at me, his expression changing from one of pure malice to something softer. Something with more of his trademark smile.

"My turn yet, doll?" His lips kicked up a notch, my All-American jock back in place.

"Not until tomorrow." I turned away, unable to reconcile the mean with the kind. The fighter with the friend. It was all too much, too fast. Too...confusing.

But Tripp didn't let me hide from him for long. He pressed against my back, wedging me between his big body and the counter, letting his hand brush my breast as he leaned in close. "You sure you want to wait?"

Flirting. I could handle flirting.

"Would you like it if I left your bed early to go be with someone else?" I sighed as he tweaked my nipple, unable to stop the shiver that swept up my body.

"Point taken. But Quinn's not here, so I'm allowed to play. Yes?"

I didn't get to answer him—though I was pretty damn sure I was going to say yes—because Quinn came stomping down the stairs. His hair was one big, wild nest, his clothes completely rumpled. And his glasses. They sat crooked again as if he'd thrown them on as an afterthought. My naughty professor before me, the sexy college quarterback behind me. The best of both worlds.

"Hey, sweet girl." Quinn leaned across the counter to place a kiss on my cheek. "Meathead here bothering you?"

Tripp gave my breast one final tweak before stepping back, resting his hip against the counter and looking like the cocky man I knew him to be. "Ha-ha-ha, fucker. Must be nice to be able to have a real girl instead of just watching all that hentai porn shit you usually jack off to."

Quinn smiled. "It is, yeah. And you don't get to find out how nice until tomorrow."

He grabbed my hand and dragged me toward the stairs. But something Tripp had said kept bouncing around in my mind. Something intriguing. Titillating. I tugged Quinn to a stop before we reached the top of the stairs, cocking my head when he turned and gave me a questioning look.

"You watch hentai porn?"

He froze, staring down at me with the most shocked expression on his face. "Well, yeah. I do."

I passed him on the stairs, stopping when my face was level with his. When I could lean in and whisper against his lips. "Why haven't we watched any together?"

Shock changed to wonder. "Fucking perfect for us."

And then he yanked me the rest of the way up the stairs and dragged me toward his wall of monitors.

Chapter Twenty-Four

"**S**o," I said as Quinn herded me across the attic. "Tripp knows you watch hentai porn."

He settled into the beanbag chair and pulled me down to sit on his lap, shoving me this way and that until he had me the way he wanted me—sprawled over his body with my legs spread on either side of his. Just like Liam had held me the night of our little show. Just like our first time fucking in that exact same spot.

"Does that surprise you?"

"No, but what does is that you wouldn't have told me about that. Why are you holding out on me?"

He leaned forward enough to drop a kiss to my lips, a hungry sort of moan vibrating through his chest. When he pulled back, his glasses were crooked again, and I had the utmost joy in watching him straighten the black frames.

"I'm sort of surprised you know about hentai porn. It's not the most popular thing out there."

I shrugged, watching as he typed something on his keyboard. "No, but that's where all the tentacle porn lives."

"Fuck, Waverley. *Fuck*." He slid his hand up and over my breast, his fingers pinching my nipple nice and hard. "Really? Tentacles?"

I groaned, arching into him. "Yes. I like the...overtaking concept of it all. Reminds me of my stallions, actually. Too big and strong to say no to —not that I'd want to say no in the first place."

"You could, you know." He nuzzled my neck, biting me once. Licking away the sting. "You could say no to any or all of us. Everything is about what you want."

"I know." I turned enough to look him in the face, running one hand up into his messy hair. "I want things to be about what *all of us* want, though. And right now, I have a feeling you want to watch porn with me."

Quinn quirked his lips into a sort of grin. "I do."

"Good, because *I want* to see what gets you off. See? We can both get exactly what we want."

He stared down at me before attacking my mouth again, slicking his tongue against mine. Making me tremble and moan before breaking away to shift his focus to his keyboard. "You really are so goddamned perfect for us, do you know that, sweet girl? So perfect."

I did. I knew it, just as I knew they were all so perfect for me. I didn't need to tell him that, though. I showed him instead. Rubbing my ass all over his lap to tease him. Bringing my arms up over my head to pull him closer, to give him a good look down my shirt—his shirt, technically—so he could see how tight my nipples were beneath the thin fabric. So he could know how much he turned me on. I rocked and rolled and dry-humped his cock until he finally grabbed my hips and stopped me.

"Behave."

I grinned. "Never."

He placed a smacking kiss on my lips, then went back to typing, his eyes bouncing between screens until they all changed. A porn website opened up, showing the last eight videos watched by his account. I was familiar with the site—knew that if he scrolled down, it would keep showing videos he'd watched. But there was also a favorites icon with the number twelve next to it. He had videos starred to rewatch.

"Show me your favorites," I said, rubbing my hands up and down his thighs. Breathless and excited to see such a personal side of him

Quinn clicked a button, and the screen changed.

I stared at the titles, my eyes bouncing from one to the next as I tried to get a feel for his preferences. "These are the ones you watch the most?"

"Yeah, I guess."

"You guess?"

He leaned forward, growling in my ear. "Sometimes, you want something specific, you know?"

I did know. My own starred videos were a mishmash of different kinks and pairings. Things I might want to watch again at some point, or videos I watched almost weekly.

One video on his screen caught my eye, and I couldn't resist. I took over the keyboard, using the trackpad to move the cursor until I could click on the title. Until that particular video filled the screens.

A woman knelt before a man, both naked, while she held her breasts together. He fucked her tits, groaning and whispering corny lines as the woman stared up at him with a fake smile on her face. Not exactly the highest quality video, but I loved a good tittie-fucking scene. Loved it more than I probably should have. Something about all the power the woman had even while on her knees got to me, though. Something about him taking the pleasure she so willingly gave made me tingle.

Quinn seemed to agree.

As he watched the couple on-screen, he groaned and grabbed my arms, tugging me back against him. Reaching around to tweak my nipples and grip my breasts nice and hard. I'd called him as a breast man when he couldn't stop staring at mine. Apparently, I'd been right.

"You like this one?" I asked as I reached behind me to palm his dick.

Quinn nodded, thrusting up into my hand. "It feeds a particular fantasy of mine."

I spun, facing him, dropping to my knees on the floor and holding myself up with my hands on his thighs. "Feeds a fantasy? Is that shorthand for gets you off while you dream about fucking some girl's tits?"

"My hand on my cock gets me off. That playing in the background is just a bonus." He grabbed my chin, looking so serious. "And the only tits I want to fuck are yours."

"So why don't you?" I grabbed the waistband of his sweats, pulling them slowly over his hips. Peeling them off him. He lifted his hips, helping me out, sitting deeper into his beanbag chair once I'd stripped him and set his cock free. Casual, never breaking his heated stare, he grabbed hold of his dick and started stroking from root to tip. Slowly. So, so slowly.

"You going to fulfill my fantasy, sweet girl?"

Yes. I pulled my shirt off and tossed it to the side before grabbing my breasts and lifting them together. "Got any lube?"

His lips lifted into my favorite, naughty grin as he leaned over and grabbed a small bottle from the drawer in the side table. "What are you planning, dirty girl?"

"You know exactly what I'm planning." I grabbed the bottle and poured a small amount of lube into my palm. Instead of using it on my skin, I reached for Quinn's cock, running my hand up and down the length of it as I held his gaze. His eyes darkened, and his breathing sped up with every pass. Every swirl of my palm over the tip. His hips rolled as I ran my thumb along the slit, as I wrapped my hand around the head and squeezed.

"You ready?" I asked, moving into position and holding my tits together. For him. To give him this fantasy of his.

He grinned again, leaning down to plant a kiss to my lips. "I'm ready for anything you're willing to give me."

I leaned in, squeezing my breasts tight as he directed his cock to the underside. As he pushed forward, slipping between them. Thrust up into the space created by my holding them together. He grunted and moaned as he watched the tip appear and disappear, as he carefully, tentatively fucked my cleavage. But that wasn't enough for me. I needed more. Needed to *give him* more.

I needed to see him lose control again.

On his next thrust, I leaned down to run my tongue over the tip of his cock. He grunted, jerking. Fucking a little harder. And on every thrust, every time the head of his cock broke through my cleavage, I licked or kissed or sucked it into my mouth. Moaning when the lube disappeared and I finally tasted pure Quinn. Shaking as he fucked into me harder, faster. As he gripped my shoulders tight and snapped his hips.

As he finally came with a groan, partially buried in my tits. Partially sucked into my mouth.

I swallowed all that I could, but it was too much and the angle was all wrong. A small thread of come leaked from my lips, dripping down my chin. Quinn stared at me, running a thumb over my lips when I finally released him, rubbing his come into my skin.

"This is the filthiest thing I've ever seen, and I've watched some of that tentacle porn myself."

I laughed, climbing onto his lap and straddling him. Kissing him deeply and rocking over him. "Did I fulfill your tittie-fucking fantasy okay?"

"Jesus, sweet girl. You rocked that." He chuckled, his eyes bright. "Now tell me, what can I do for you? What do you want from your mate?"

Damn, I loved it when he called himself my mate.

"Make me come," I whispered against his lips. "Your hand, your mouth, your cock—doesn't matter. Just make me come."

And he did.

Multiple times.

All night long.

Chapter Twenty-Five

I woke up alone in Quinn's bed, the buzz of conversation from across the attic pulling me from sleep to wakefulness in seconds.

"Far west pasture. Camera eight. Cade's on his way."

I slipped out of bed, following Quinn's voice. Padding down the hallway in my bare feet with Quinn's sheet wrapped around me. I spotted Liam first, standing behind Quinn, his face set in a scowl and his arms crossed over his broad chest.

"How long?"

Quinn typed madly, shaking his head. "Can't tell exactly. Close to two hours, it looks like."

"Two hours? How the fuck was he able to make that camera loop for two hours without us noticing?"

Him. By the vicious tone of Liam's voice, he had to mean Chance.

"What's going on?" I asked, coming around the corner and letting them both see me. "And don't give me some bullshit, 'we're taking care of it' brush-off."

Liam gave me a weak smile. "We're taking care of it, but that's not a brush-off."

"Someone looped a video on one of our new security cameras. We're missing almost two hours of footage." Quinn sighed, running a hand through his messy hair. "I need to pull all the backups. No fucking way did he get past my systems."

Quinn was up and off to the far side of the room in seconds, sliding into a rolling desk chair and typing on another computer. One I hadn't even noticed.

"What is he doing?"

Liam came up behind me, wrapping an arm around my shoulders. "Protecting you, sugar. What we're all doing."

"How can I help?"

"You help just by being here."

I turned, looking up at him, hanging on to his thick arms. "I want to do more."

"Liam," Cade's voice sounded through a speaker, making the man before me go from my sweet Liam to the protector. The lion.

"Hang on, Waverley." He moved to the side table, pressing a key on the keyboard. "Go ahead, Cade."

"We definitely had an intruder. I've got footprints underneath the tree where the camera's mounted."

"Leading toward the house?"

"No. Coming in from the far west pasture and walking back out that way. Nothing toward the house."

Liam frowned, his heavy brow furrowing. "Are you sure?"

"Absolutely. We need to run a camera check on the others that are up and running, but I'm not sure we'll get anything out this far. Garrett's circling the property with Matthew now—he'll need someone on camera duty to verify the cameras are all working normally."

Liam looked to where Quinn sat working. "I'll do that. Call for me instead of Quinn."

"Roger. I'll let them know."

"You following the footprints?"

"Fuck yeah," Cade said, sounding way too excited. "Dalton's like a hunting dog on a lead waiting for me to be ready to go."

Definitely way too excited.

Liam nodded as if the man on the other end of the radio could see him. "Get on it, then. And keep in fucking touch. No one goes out alone."

"Same to you. Keep our precious little fox secure."

Liam winked at me. "Roger that."

As soon as Liam closed the line, I grabbed him. Needing to touch, to feel. To steal some comfort from him. "Let me help. Let me do something."

Liam leaned down and planted a soft kiss to my lips before turning me to face Quinn. "He's going to be beating himself up all night about the camera thing even though he wasn't the one scheduled to monitor the feed. Go. Take care of him. That will be the biggest help for all of us."

He pushed me softly, starting me on the path toward my naughty professor. Not that I needed the help. My poor Quinn looked completely out of sorts. His shoulders sat stiff, his head shaking as he pounded on the keyboard and stared at the screen before him.

When I finally reached him, I grabbed his shoulders, massaging away the tension. Trying to, at least. "What can I do?"

He sighed and clutched my hand, pulling it to his mouth to kiss the palm. "Just sit with me. Okay, sweet girl? I need to know you're safe."

I nodded and crawled into his lap, wrapping myself around him as he continued looking for...whatever he was looking for. But it was already so late, and we'd had a physically exhausting day. The warmth of his chest against my cheek and the rhythmic click of the keys made me drowsy no matter how hard I tried to fight it. I found myself falling deeper into a sleepy state as the time went on. He didn't seem to mind, simply adjusted his position so I could rest my head on his shoulder.

At least until he jumped up and hollered.

"Got you, you fucking bastard."

I nearly fell off his lap, sitting straight up, my eyes darting immediately to the screen.

And this time, I screamed.

Chance's face took up the width of the monitor, a dark, heavy hat on his head as if he'd been trying to hide beneath it. I couldn't stop the tremble that shook me, the fear that tightened my throat and made my breath come too fast.

He was here.

On Hidden E property.

He'd come for me.

Quinn grabbed my chin and forced me to look away, holding me tight. "Sorry, sweet girl. I didn't mean to wake you."

"Everything okay?" Liam appeared behind Quinn, looking worried.

"Yeah. I got a little excited and woke up Sleeping Beauty here."

"You weren't the thing that scared me." I pointed at the screen. "Chance."

Liam scowled. "Motherfucker. You found the unlooped feed?"

"Yeah. The guy's got some tech experience—that splice was a good one. It even overrode the backup drives. But I found a copy of the original feed that had video right up until he fucked with it."

"Good job, Quinn. Cade and Dalton followed the tracks but lost them at the creek. They can review the tape and formulate a timeline for when that bastard was on our property."

"I can do it," Quinn said, reaching for the keyboard again even as he yawned. That wouldn't do. Thankfully, my other stallion seemed to agree with me.

"No." Liam settled a hand on Quinn's shoulder, giving me a wink. "Go to bed. Protect our girl. We've got this, brother."

I smiled up at Liam, knowing a good night's rest was exactly what Quinn needed. He could start fresh in the morning, dig deep into his data and drives to find more information. The others could back him up for a few more hours.

"C'mon, Quinn." I grabbed his hand, tugging him out of the chair. Holding him upright when he wobbled. "You're exhausted. Let me take you to bed."

Quinn didn't argue. Instead, he followed me down the hall to his bedroom. Once I had him behind closed doors, I stripped him of his clothes, running my hands over his tired muscles. Massaging him softly. There was nothing sexual about my actions—this was about care and concern. Intimacy. Making sure my mate had what he needed.

And what he needed was rest.

He was half asleep before his head hit the pillow, but he still reached for me. Pulled me in close and wrapped his body around mine. Held me tight as he kissed my shoulder and slid his hands over my back and ass.

"Thank you, sweet girl."

"For what?"

"Showing up."

I couldn't help but smile. "Well, thanks for being here when I finally made it to the ranch."

"Tripp's going to wake us up at the ass-crack of dawn, you know," he mumbled.

Tripp. My jock. The next in line to spend time with me. As much as I liked my day with my naughty professor, I couldn't help but look forward to what was next.

To spending time with the rest of my stallions.

"I'll try to keep him from waking you up." I grinned, wiggling in Quinn's hold.

"Sleep, Waverley," he said, rolling me halfway underneath him. "I need you rested."

My heart jumped. "For when Chance comes?"

"No, for when you do. I intend to wake you up with my face between those gorgeous thighs once I grab a quick nap."

"Quinn, be serious."

"I am. There are six men downstairs right now making sure you're safe. So rest while you can and enjoy every second. We've got you."

And they did. I knew it.

But I also knew Chance wouldn't give up. He was coming for me, had already been on Hidden E property.

And my stallions were the only things standing in his way.

Chapter Twenty-Six

I woke up craving cinnamon buns and an iced coffee with extra cream and sugar. What I got instead was a roller coaster ride thanks to Tripp.

"What the... Put me down!" I hollered, laughing as Tripp jostled me around. I hadn't been fully awake when the big lug had barged into Quinn's bedroom. Hadn't yet gotten out of bed when he'd yanked the covers off me. I hadn't even been wearing any clothes when he'd tossed me over his broad shoulder and carried me out of the bedroom. Tripp didn't seem to care about all of that. The man had his big hand settled firmly on my bare ass as he carried me across Quinn's attic and toward the stairs.

"I'm not listening to you, doll. It's my turn today, Quinn. Enjoy your porn."

Quinn looked up from where he sat at his computer, shooting me a quick smile. "I definitely will. Especially the homemade ones."

I'd like to say I blushed, but how could I? Those videos we'd made were hot as hell—I sort of wanted all my stallions to see them just so I could watch their reactions. Herd movie night? I needed to get that on the schedule.

Tripp laughed all the way down the stairs and into the kitchen, where he set me on my feet in front of the island. Garrett sat at the table, while Cade and Dalton stood off to one side, chatting. At least, they were until Tripp exploded into the room with my ass in his hand. All of them turned to stare at us...more specifically, at me. I was still so very naked.

"What do you want for breakfast?" Tripp asked, his light eyes bright and his smile unstoppable.

I wasn't quite as excited as him. I leaned in close, using his body to shield mine. "Can I get a shirt?"

His brow furrowed, his confusion clear. "Is that a weird name for some funky dessert thing?"

"No. I don't have any clothes on, and I would like *a shirt.*"

His confusion melted into a look of lust, and he made it a point to drag his gaze up and down my body. "I'd hate to cover up something so pretty, doll."

Smooth talker. He didn't refuse me, though. In fact, the man stripped off his own plain, white tee. And oh my stars, was that man a work of art. A study in the beauty of masculine musculature. It wasn't the first time I'd seen him shirtless—my stallions tended to be extremely comfortable with their bodies, as well they should have been—but the view still stopped me in my tracks. I had to take a moment—just a few seconds— to admire what the fates had given me when they'd picked this man as one of my mates.

Tall and broad, Tripp towered over me. The dark hair that all my stallions sported was a bit longer on Tripp than the rest of the herd, his eyes a bit more crystalline. Muscles upon muscles thickened his arms and lined his abdomen, and a darker trail of hair led from his navel past the waistband of his basketball shorts. His very tented basketball shorts. Happy trail, indeed.

I took the shirt he offered—ignoring his cocky grin—and tugged it on. I also ignored the slickness between my thighs and the thrum of my heart racing in my chest. Not that every shifter in the room couldn't smell me, couldn't hear how fast my heart beat. They all knew and probably would have enjoyed watching me fall apart right there in the kitchen under Tripp's hands. Me? I needed sustenance before I ended up in another stallion's bed.

Breakfast first. Then... Well, I really hoped Tripp had plans for us.

"What's on the menu this morning, boys?" I asked, holding up a hand before they got any ideas that might make me rethink my plans. "Not me. Real food."

"Damn, beautiful," Garrett said, shooting me the sexiest smile known to man. "One night with Quinn, and you put the kibosh on pre-breakfast sexing? That's so harsh."

"She's building up her energy for me. She knows I'm going to wear her out." Tripp smacked my ass and headed for the refrigerator. "Omelets okay? We've got some leftover stuff from the other night we can bulk them up with."

"Sure," Garrett said as Cade sat down at the table with him. "I could go for omelets."

"Absolutely... Need some help?" Dalton slipped in behind me, hanging on to my hips and rubbing his very hard dick against my ass as he moved past me. "Excuse me, princess."

Not helping the slick thighs situation.

"No problem," I said, looking up at him over my shoulder. "And good morning, handsome."

"Good morning. How about you go settle in with Cade and Garrett? Let old Tripp and me take care of you."

"Who you calling old?" Tripp asked. Dalton tapped my ass, sending me toward the table across the room.

"Get over here, sweet girl." Garrett grinned and patted his lap. I practically skipped over, curling up in his arms as two of my seven stallions started cooking. Quinn had stayed upstairs, which meant Liam and Matthew were...somewhere else.

"Where are the other two?"

Tripp glanced at Dalton before saying, "They're outside. Tracking."

Because of my ex having been on their property. "Oh."

The happy bubble I'd woken up in burst, and the anxiety that had been slowly growing within me exploded. My men were in danger because of me. Because of my bad decisions. I hated it—hated knowing they were exhausting themselves guarding the farm. Hated knowing there was nothing I could do but sit and wait for the worst.

I hated all of it.

"Wow, you just got super tense." Garrett ran a hand up and down my spine, slipping under my shirt to touch my bare skin. "Hey, Tripp—switch spots with me."

Tripp hurried over, and the two handed me off as if I were a parcel instead of a person. Not that I minded. Either way, I was in the strong arms of one of my stallions, which was all I wanted.

"Easy, doll. Stop worrying about us. We've got this shit handled."

"What if I don't want you all to have to handle it?"

"We don't always get what we want. Unless it's something you're asking for in bed, then you get everything."

"You have a one-track mind."

Tripp shifted under me, letting me feel how hard he was. "I have a sexy-as-sin mate in my arms. One I've seen come on a herd mate's fingers but haven't gotten a taste of myself. I can't help myself."

I wished I could say his words made me feel better, but I couldn't. I was too worked up—too anxious. My fox paced inside my head, chittering away. Needing to bust out and run. To escape from my mind and let the fresh air ruffle her fur.

"Can we go for a run today?" I asked, staring out the window with something close to longing making my heart hurt.

Cade and Dalton answered immediately and in unison. "Fuck no."

My entire body shuddered at their refusal. Luckily, Tripp wasn't so hard and unrelenting.

"Maybe," he said, still holding me tightly. Still trying to soothe the fear inside of me. "Let's wait for Matthew and Liam to come back, and then we'll figure something out. In the meantime, we'll eat and have some fun."

That wouldn't be enough for my fox to settle, but I nodded anyway. "Okay."

We finished breakfast in a quiet sort of tension, me staring out the window more and more as the guys stared at anything but me. I had a feeling they didn't like seeing me disappointed, seeing me want something they couldn't give me, but I couldn't help myself. My fox grew more upset with every minute inside, which threw my own nervousness into overdrive. If we couldn't get outside for a run, we needed a distraction.

Thankfully, Tripp seemed to understand that. As soon as we were once again alone in the kitchen, he pulled me into his arms, his chest to my back, and kissed his way down the length of my neck. His hands soft but his cock hard against me.

"Nothing will happen to you or us. Not today, not tomorrow, not ever. We've got you, and we'll do everything in our power to keep you happy and healthy." He spun me around to place a soft, sweet kiss on my lips. One that quickly turned heated as he grabbed my ass and pulled me up the length of his body. He had me pinned to the front of the refrigerator in seconds, had his hand between us and stroking my pussy right after. His mouth owning mine in a deep, wet kiss that muddled every thought I had. I'd needed a distraction, and he was a perfect one. All hard and hot and ready for me to lose myself in for a few hours.

"C'mon, doll," he said when he finally pulled away. "It's our day together, and I won't let this bullshit ruin it. Let's go have some fun."

He smacked my ass, tossed me back over his shoulder, and carried me down the hall, singing loudly the entire way. Making me laugh. Making me forget...just for a moment.

Chapter Twenty-Seven

Fun in the world of Tripp meant hanging out in his room. Considering he had an air hockey table taking up the center of it and a wall of board games, I couldn't blame him for having a ball while in there. Playing games with him was the distraction I needed to let go of my anxiety and just...be me.

"You're going down." He grinned and flicked his wrist hard, sending the puck flying my way across the smooth surface of the table. I blocked it—barely—and laughed.

"I'll happily go down all night long for you, hot stuff. Just as soon as I kick your ass at this game."

Tripp flicked his gaze my way but only for a second. "Offering to suck my dick won't help you, doll. I've got a one-track mind, and it's focused on winning right now."

Maybe. Maybe not. He'd been teasing me all morning, walking around without his shirt and with that monster of an erection in his shorts. The one my pussy had been clenching for, wanting to be filled with, for hours.

Air hockey was fun and all, but I was ready for more.

I smacked my paddle down the next time the puck came my way, stopping it. "How about we up the ante here? Make this game a little more interesting."

Tripp gave me a grin. "What did you have in mind?"

"Strip air hockey. First to miss a shot takes it off."

"We're both only wearing one layer. That'd be an awfully short game."

That's what I'm hoping for. I shrugged. "If you're not interested in getting me naked—"

Tripp's laugh practically exploded out of him. "Not interested in getting you naked? I've been jacking myself raw since you showed up here. It's about time I retire old Rosy Palm."

Jackpot. I leaned over the game, biting my lip and sending him what I hoped was a saucy wink. "You're the one who wanted to play this game instead of jumping right into something more...physical."

"Only because you seemed to need the distraction." He rapped his knuckles against the play surface. "C'mon, let's get this over with so I can get you naked again. That little peek this morning wasn't nearly enough."

I launched the puck at him, laughing when he made an exaggerated block. We continued back and forth for a few minutes, neither of us willing to throw the game, both of us laughing the entire time. But then my stallion made one hell of a shot, and the puck came screaming into my goal. Completely unstoppable. Game over.

Or maybe it was just beginning.

"There you go, doll. Looks like it's time for you to give me back my shirt. And don't even think about trying to talk your way out of it."

I raised an eyebrow and took a step back, making sure he could see the length of me before pulling his shirt over my head. I dropped it to the floor and cocked a hip. "I would never *not* follow through on a bet."

He slipped around the edge of the table, his eyes definitely not looking at mine. "You sure you're ready for this, little doll? I'm not going to be gentle."

As if I would ever ask him to be. "Game on, Tripp."

He was on me in a flash, growling as he took my mouth in a punishing kiss. So hot and warm before me. So strong as he grabbed my thighs and lifted me, pinning me to the wall with his thick body.

Groaning into my mouth as I wrapped my legs around his waist and rocked my hips against him.

"Your pussy that needy, little one?" he asked, grunting and pressing his thick, hard length against me. "You want me to fill that wet cunt with my cock? Want me to fuck up into you until you're screaming my name?"

I gasped and dropped my head against his shoulder, the explosions of sensation rocking the very foundation of my mind. "You seem awfully cocky, Tripp. I don't scream often."

He chuckled. "Bullshit. I've heard you. I've had to reach into my pants and jack myself off every fucking day because of listening to you come. It's my turn to make you holler."

Without any sign of strain, he practically threw me up the wall, lifting me until my knees were spread around his shoulders. Until he had my hips placed so my pussy was right in front of his face. Goodness, the man was strong. So very strong.

And hungry.

He dove into my pussy like a man possessed, sucking hard on my clit from the get-go. No pausing, no teasing or preparation...just direct action. Suction right where I wanted it most. He was on a mission to get me off, and I was all in on that plan.

I grabbed his hair, tugging hard as he increased the pressure. "Oh, Tripp. Like that. Like that. You're going to make me come so fast."

He groaned and sucked harder, assaulting my clit. Lashing at it with his tongue before suckling me deep. No fingers inside me, nothing for my pussy to clench down on, but there wasn't anything more he needed to do. His mouth was plenty talented.

The pressure of my impending release built within me, hot and strong and like nothing ever before. Something about the way he worked me over, about the way his mouth owned my clit, made the tingles signaling what was to come so much stronger. Deeper. Different. Oh my, this was *so* different. I had no idea what was coming, but I wanted it. Needed to feel it, had to know—

Three fingers plunging inside me with no warning from Tripp and a hard press to my G-spot did me in. Sent sensations I'd never experienced shooting through me and intensifying the moment. With a scream and a gush of heat between my legs, I came harder than ever before. One arm raised, my hand pressing into the wall behind me, elbow bumping the high ceiling, the other holding him to me. My fingers twisted in his hair and clung hard as my entire body locked down into my release. As I shook and shuddered...and soaked him.

What the devil?

"That's it, doll," Tripp said, teasing me with his fingers pressed deep and his thumb rolling over my clit. "A little more. I know you've got it in you."

"Did I..." I rocked against him, groaning as another wave of release washed over me. As the wet, squelching sounds of his fingers inside me grew louder. "Oh god, why am I so wet?"

"You squirted. It's so fucking hot, little doll. I just want to lick up every drop." He punctuated his point by giving me an exaggerated lick from my inner thigh all the way up to the lips of my pussy. "I want to feel that while you're riding my cock."

I couldn't even imagine. I'd felt that orgasm in the deepest parts of myself—places I hadn't known existed. I had no idea what would happen if he gave me more.

I was totally ready to find out, though.

"Can we try that now?"

Tripp grinned, pulling me from the wall and carrying me to his bed. "You want my cock already?"

No teasing necessary. Not with Tripp. Not with any of my stallions.

"Yes. I want to feel you inside me." As soon as he laid me down, I rocked against him, rubbing myself along the front of his silky shorts. Likely soaking him. "I need you to fill me up."

Tripp groaned and reached between us, shucking his shorts with ease before spreading my legs. Pulling one knee up and over his shoulder to open me wider for him. Lining himself up with my entrance.

"My mate needs cock," he whispered, almost seeming to talk to himself. "Aren't I the lucky stallion to get to fulfill that for her?"

"Tripp, please." I grabbed at his shoulders, trying to move him. To pull him inside. He just grinned down at me. Rocking slowly. Teasing.

"You think you can take me, Waverley? You think you're ready for me to fuck this slick cunt?"

Damn, I loved his dirty mouth. "Yes. Yes, Tripp. Please."

He slid inside me, only an inch or so. Barely the tip. "I don't know. You just squirted all over my face. I don't think you're ready for more yet. I don't want to break this pussy. I have so many plans for it. For you." He leaned down, kissing me softly. Sweetly. So out of context with his words. "I have plans for us."

I liked the idea of an *us* because I knew he meant all of us—my herd of stallions and me. Full count of eight on that us.

"All of us," I said, kissing him back. "I need a night with all my men."

"You do. But not tonight. Tonight's mine." He thrust inside me, no longer teasing. Groaning loudly as he paused balls deep. As he held himself so stiff, filling me to the point of pain, stretching me as I squirmed and gasped and dug my fingers into his flesh. "Fuck, this pussy is heaven. Absolutely heaven. So tight and hot. So wet."

And he was so very thick. "Move, Tripp. Please move."

So he did. Hard and rough, not taking it easy on me. Fucking me up the bed with his big body, his thick cock. His filthy fucking mouth.

"Your cunt's sucking me in, doll. So greedy, aren't you? So needy. Can't get deep enough, can I? You just keep wanting more. Look at you, clenching on me already. I'm going to make you come again with hardly any effort. Gonna have you squirting all over my cock."

I loved that idea—wanted to feel that deep, aching sort of need be relieved again. Wanted to know how him being buried inside me, stretching me with his girth, would make it better. If that was even possible.

Instead of finishing me off, though, Tripp pulled out—sliding me down the mattress. Flipping me over so he could fuck up into me from behind. So he could bend me over and pin me down with his big body. Thrusting deeper than before. Slipping his fingers between my legs to pinch my clit.

So he could lift his hand and bring it down hard, slapping my pussy as he drove himself all the way inside. Sensations exploded, blinding me. Making it impossible to do anything but feel the pleasure overtake me. Tripp made me come so hard that I felt the contractions along every single inch of my body. Just like before—deeper than I'd ever known— and so, so good.

This time, instead of his face, I soaked his cock *and* his bed.

Tripp fucked me through all of it, grunting in my ear and driving himself harder than before. Speeding up and losing rhythm until he finally pressed deep, holding himself still as he groaned and came inside me. As he filled me with his come and added to the sloppy mess I'd become.

"Fuck, Waverley. You're so goddamned hot." He rocked through his own orgasm, seated deep within me, breathing hard. "We're going to need one of those plastic sheets. I'm never going to get enough of you soaking me like this."

I should have been embarrassed—we really had made a mess—but I couldn't be bothered about it. He'd drawn that out of me—had made me come so hard, I'd lost control of everything else. Made my body go crazy on his tongue and fingers.

And if a plastic sheet meant he'd do it again, I was all in.

Chapter Twenty-Eight

Tripp liked to read.

That really shouldn't have surprised me as much as it did. All my stallions seemed intelligent, but for some reason, Tripp's wild personality and love of sports had left me making assumptions about him. Ones I now felt bad about. The man had more books in his room than the other stallions. Precarious piles forming tables and stacks, hidden columns under chairs and dressers. Tucked into every corner were more and more books, and as soon as we had cleaned up from our sex-a-thon, he pulled one out and began to read it to me.

My guilt at assuming he was *just a jock* weighed me down, though—making it almost impossible to enjoy the moment. Tripp was smart, not just muscular. Witty, not just athletic. And he was mine.

"You okay, doll?"

Was I? I had no idea. My thoughts kept circling, fluttering around in my head and bringing waves of emotions I wasn't sure if I was ready to handle. The idea of being with my men, my stallion herd, brought me more joy and peace than I'd ever imagined possible. The idea of losing them? Of hurting one of them with my words or deeds...with my past? Of anything bad ever happening to even one of them?

Horrifying.

When I didn't answer right away, Tripp rolled me into his arms, setting his book down behind me and nuzzling my neck. "Talk to me."

"I'm just thinking."

"About what?"

"You. Us. This. The herd."

He hummed against me, licking up the column of my neck before whispering, "Don't worry. I won't tell the others I'm your favorite."

I chuckled, snuggling deeper. Loving the fun side of Tripp and how he made me find joy even in my most tumultuous moments. "You're awfully full of yourself."

"In this herd? I have to be."

That comment had a depth to it. I'd never thought of Tripp as anything other than confident, but that statement—the tone in his voice —made me wonder. It also made me think about my seven stallions. "Every one of you is so different."

"We are. We each have our place and our jobs, the assigned duties and the unassigned ones."

"Unassigned?"

"Like Garrett—he's the farrier of the group, did you know that? Handles all the issues with putting shoes on the horses and dealing with their hooves. That's his assigned job, but his *unassigned* one is to make sure the entire herd—shifting and non-shifting horses—is healthy and strong, both physically and mentally. He supports us all, you know?"

I did. I'd seen that with him, the way he worried and showed his concern. How he took care of them all. "He's good at it."

"He is. And Liam keeps us all working together while running the business. Matthew is the heavy when we need one. He trains the horses as well."

I hadn't given the structure of the herd enough thought. Hadn't realized there were so many nuances to it. Now that I had, I wanted to know everything. "What's your job?"

"I'm a veterinarian."

That pulled me up short. "Really?"

"Yep. But when I'm not doing that, I make sure everyone relaxes. I bring the fun." He rolled me over, settling between my thighs once again. Leaning down to suck my nipple into his mouth as I grabbed his hair and sighed. Loving his attention, his touch. Everything about being with him.

Tripp rocked against me, teasing me slowly. In no rush, it seemed. Taking his time as he lavished my nipples with attention. Eventually, he popped off my breast, rising over me with a smile on his chiseled face. "You need to relax more."

I arched as he thrust inside me, as he held my gaze and slid into my pussy. Deep. So, so deep and slow and perfect. He watched me as he moved back and forth. As he filled me with his hard cock. That stare, that connection between us, rocked me harder than anything his body did to me could. This wasn't about sex—none of my men would ever be able to convince me our connections were only physical. Our emotions had become tangled too. Had locked us together forever.

Maybe that was why I couldn't breathe. Maybe the fear of losing the greatest gift I'd ever been given was the reason my heart refused to settle into a steady rhythm.

Maybe the possibility of a disruption in my herd was why the ache inside me continued to grow.

"What is it, doll?" Tripp stopped with his cock buried inside me and a frown on his face. "What's on your mind?"

Liam. Matthew. Garrett. Quinn. Cade. Dalton. And yes, my Tripp. My seven stallions. The mates I hadn't seen coming but whom I'd do anything for. The men I'd lost my heart to. My new world.

But how could I say all that?

"I worry," I said, keeping my voice low. Soft. My throat thick with all the things I couldn't put into words.

Tripp seemed to hear what I didn't say, though. "I know you do, but you don't have to. We won't let anything bad happen." He slid deeper, grinding against my clit. Keeping his blue eyes locked on mine as we joined physically. Emotionally. Soulfully.

"Tripp. What is this? Why do things feel so different?"

He shook his head, groaning as his movements sped up. As the pressure grew. As I clung to his shoulders and held on for dear life.

"You're ours," he said, dropping down to wrap me in his arms.

Holding me with a strength that should have been painful. "We've finally found you, and we won't let you go. We've got you, doll."

But who had them?

Chapter Twenty-Nine

Lunch was a much quieter affair than usual, primarily because I spent it alone with Tripp. Not a hardship, but I would have liked to have seen my other men. The worry for them—the fear—it ate at me. Growing stronger as the hours passed without them near. Taking over my every waking thought.

"Not liking the chicken salad?" Tripp asked, motioning toward my virtually untouched plate. "I could grab some apples or raisins for it to add some sweetness."

I gave him a smile, trying hard to put on a brave face. "Raisins don't belong in other food, and I'm not the biggest fan of apples."

Tripp sat back, big, green apple in hand, looking all sorts of nonchalant. And male. The way his arms bulged even in such a casual pose? The spread of his legs as he took up space. The man was quite the specimen. "If you're not hungry enough for an apple, you're not hungry enough."

He took a giant bite of his apple, smiling around it. I shrugged.

"My mom used to say that about doughnuts."

His eyes went wide, and his chewing slowed. Finally, he shook his head with a laugh. "Such a fox."

"Guilty as charged. And the chicken salad is fine, I was just thinking about the herd."

The man could recognize serious time like no one else. His smile dropped, his body language changing. Leaning closer to me as if he knew I needed that. "You miss them."

So much. "Is it wrong? I know it's our day to get to know one another better—"

"Nothing you could want with us would ever be wrong unless you *didn't* want anything with us. That would definitely be an issue because we all want you so damn much, doll." He snagged me by the waist and pulled me into his lap, cuddling me against his chest. "I miss them too, you know."

"You do?"

"I do. We're tight. We work together, live together, and play together. It's hard not to be around them as much as I'm used to. Maybe after—"

"Tripp, we need you." Cade came rushing in, looking big and dirty and as close to showing an emotion as I'd ever seen him. "One of the mares looks to be colicking. Liam's got her on her feet, but—"

"On it." Tripp didn't give him a chance to finish his sentence. He smacked a kiss to my lips, pushed me back into my own chair, and was racing out the door before I even got to say goodbye. He obviously took his job as veterinarian of the herd seriously. There was something really attractive about that.

There was also something attractive about the hulking menace of a man staring me down from the doorway.

The one I had yet to get to know. "Are you hungry, Cade? You can come in and join me. I won't bite."

Cade huffed, his eyes so darn bright in the sun shining through the window. More intense than usual as well. "Not even if I tell you to?"

Oh my stars. A shiver of arousal laced with fear raced up my spine. *He and Dalton do everything together.* I shot him a smile, passing over the conversation for the moment. I could deal with him and his possible need to feel my teeth on his body tomorrow. "No Dalton today?"

"He's patrolling the perimeter. We still don't have full camera coverage on the farm and a few of the ones we do have went down, so we need to manually monitor the east field."

A few cameras down—that's what Chance had done already. Taken the cameras offline and looped the feed so he wouldn't be noticed. That was what had thrown Quinn into such a state of guilt and duty. My poor professor had been a mess at the idea that one camera had been compromised. A few would have to be killing him.

"Is Quinn okay?"

Cade's lips quirked, almost pulling into a full smile. "He's fine. His upgraded systems caught the variance in the camera feed when the perp took them out, so there was little-to-no downtime."

A ray of sunshine in the darkness my day had suddenly become. "So he's here."

Cade definitely knew I meant Chance. "He won't get close to you."

"He got close enough to mess with the cameras."

Cade didn't say anything, just stood against the doorframe and seethed. I could practically see the fury rolling off him, and I definitely felt the tension in the room as my words sat heavy and hard between us. For the second time, one of my stallions made me feel fear. That was unexpected.

"I'm sorry," I whispered, looking to the floor. Unsure how to handle the anxiety his anger caused me.

Cade didn't seem to like my apology. He stalked across the kitchen, yanking my chair out from under the table and making me yelp. Leaning over and pinning me in place as he got right in my face. So very dangerous, this man. And so very pissed off. "Don't you ever be sorry. Nothing this fucker does is your fault. This isn't on you, woman."

Woman. The word, the tone of his voice as he practically punched the air with the term, sent a shiver up my spine. Sent the warmth of arousal down deep in my gut. Sent my heart fluttering. Big and mean and dangerous...and mine. A little fear only added to the delicious tension already brewing between us.

But still, I worried about what was happening to the Hidden E and my herd. "He's here for me."

"He won't get you."

Just like the rest of the herd, Cade jumped right to the conclusion that my fear was based on self-preservation. And maybe it was, but not the way they all seemed to think. Because, of course, I feared Chance getting his hands on me, but even more than that, I worried about my stallions. About what would happen if Chance got his hands on one of *them*. Why couldn't my men understand where my worry came from?

"And if he gets one of my stallions instead?"

Cade jerked back, deep blue eyes wide as they took me in. Realization dawning over his chiseled face. "Is that what you're so worried about? That he might pick a fight with one of us?"

A fight. I was worried about so much more than a simple fight.

"What if he gets one of you alone? I watched him murder people, Cade. What if he..." I couldn't even say it. Couldn't think it. The idea of losing one of my seven, the possibility of it, tore something lose in my chest. I brought my fist to my mouth, trying hard to fight back the tears ready to burst from my body. I couldn't lose them. Any of them.

I failed miserably, though, as a sob broke free.

Cade grabbed me, pulled me right off my chair and into his strong arms. Held me like a baby as he stared down with those blue eyes I hadn't even begun to see enough of. "We all know the risks out there, and we all know what's waiting for us here at home." He walked with me, moving to set me on the edge of the island. When he had me where he wanted me, he ran a single finger down my face as if afraid to touch me more. As if unable not to. "Every one of us will do whatever it takes to remove the threat to the ranch and come back to you. That will always be our main goal—doing everything in our power to be with you. No human is going to get in the way of that, Waverley. Not ever."

Matthew walked through the door from the porch, his face drawn and a frown on his lips as he noticed our position. "Everything okay?"

"Everything's fine." Cade backed up, keeping his eyes on mine. Cocking his head a little as he regarded me. I had no idea what he saw, but whatever it was, he seemed to come to some conclusion. He nodded once before tearing his eyes from mine and looking at Matthew. "I think our girl needs to spend some time in the barn this afternoon. A day with the horses will do her good."

The horses. A day spent outside on the farm but also time with my stallions. An afternoon being able to watch all of them work, to see them in the place they seemed so comfortable, would definitely do me good. "When can we go?"

Chapter Thirty

I loved being in the barn. The big, open building was full of life and energy, the activity inside it giving me so much to enjoy. I leaned against the fence that separated the indoor arena from the stalls, watching Matthew working the horses. Running them in circles on a long leash-like thing with a whip in his hand. Cade had called the activity lunging—I called it poetry in motion. Matthew had a gentle way about him, had soft eyes and kind words for the horse on the end of the line as she ran around him. He didn't touch her with the whip either—simply brought it closer to her hip if she slowed. He made it easy for her to follow his directions and give him what he wanted—a skill that had definitely transferred into other areas of his life.

As if sensing where my thoughts had gone—to our night together and how he had made it easy for me to follow his directions as well—he looked my way. A sinful smirk danced across his lips before he went back to watching the mare. Keeping his attention where it belonged.

Liam came rushing down the hall, sidestepping when he saw me. "Well, this is a surprise. How're you doing today, sugar?"

"I'm good." I leaned into his hug, giggling when he pressed a bunch of quick kisses to my neck. "How are you? Your day going well?"

"It'd be better if I could get under this sexy little sundress you're wearing." He gripped my hips, pulling me close as he tugged up my skirt a little. Letting me feel how hard he was. For me. Always for me. "Once all this getting to know each other stuff is done, I want to take you back to the meadow. Let your sweet body soak up some sun."

"I'd like that." Like was an understatement. The last time Liam had taken me to the meadow, we'd had amazing sex in the tall grass. That had been my first time with him, the first time I'd given myself to any of my stallions. That memory felt just a little sweeter than any other because of the initial connection we'd formed.

Liam must have felt the same way. He stared down at me with a smile on his face, looking so ridiculously handsome. Watching me with something close to love in his eyes. "It's a date, then. But for now, I have to get to my office and make a few calls. You need anything?"

Only more time with my men. "I'm good."

"You're more than just good. Stay with the others, you hear?" One last kiss and Liam headed for the back of the barn.

Quinn appeared next, tablet in hand and a deep frown on his face. "Hey, sweet girl." He patted my ass and gave me a distracted kiss. "I saw you walking over with Matthew and Cade. Make sure you stay inside, okay?"

My stomach dropped. *Stay inside*—meaning outside was likely dangerous. "Yeah. Okay."

He stopped, his eyes finally meeting mine. His attention solely on me. "It's fine, you know. We've got everything covered, and there's no way this guy will come head on at us in broad daylight. This is downtime. It's just easier on me if I know exactly where to look for you."

Oh, that...wasn't as bad as I'd thought. I would do anything to make this situation easier on all of them. "I'll stay inside until Tripp's ready to take me back home. Promise."

"Good." He leaned in close, pressing his lips to mine and licking his way into my mouth before pulling back with a sigh. "You look pretty in that dress. Like some sort of naughty girl-next-door fantasy."

"We can play that one out next time. Maybe in front of the cameras so we can watch it afterward."

His grin set my heart on fire. "You're on."

Quinn headed after Liam, eyes back on his tablet, his frown a little less severe. Maybe this was my way of helping them—being present. Showing up and giving them things to look forward to. Giving them the promise of me.

I had no idea where Cade and Dalton had disappeared to, but Tripp and Garrett were working together on the far side of the barn, both bent over to look at the hoof of one of the mares. Such a sight—two glorious backsides in the air, two strong sets of thighs bunching under the tight jeans they each wore. I could have watched them all day—had already spent way too much time with my eyes glued to them and Garrett as they'd worked that afternoon. But alas, a girl couldn't fill her day with ass-staring—touching was much more fulfilling.

Heart happy, I strolled through the barn, slowly working my way toward the farrier and the veterinarian. On the way, I passed the room where the guys stored the saddles and other supplies. Something about the smell of leather, about the shininess of the metal pieces on the saddles and bridles and the organization the men employed, drew me inside.

The room sat slightly shadowed and cooler than the rest of the barn. Seeming almost like a secret hideaway. A place to be alone and gather my thoughts. Saddles rested on wooden stands that looked like little soldiers taking up floor space, and bridles hung from hooks high over my head. A veritable leather museum and a silent space filled with reverence for the tools the men used to control the thousand-plus-pound animals in their care. Such a perfect place. And so solitary.

At least until the quiet was broken by a voice that made my panties wet. "Looking to go for a ride?"

I turned, smiling at Tripp. He stood in the doorway—one heavy shoulder leaning against the frame, his arms crossed over his broad chest and a smile on his face.

Wet was an understatement. That big, hulking, beast of a man had me soaked in seconds just by looking at me. It was definitely time to play with my cocky jock.

"I've never ridden before." I bit my lip and backed up, bumping into the side of a saddle. "Are you going to teach me?"

Tripp pushed off the wall, striding closer, his gait long and loose but determined. The man looked as if he were on a mission, and if that mission had anything to do with making me crave his body on mine, he was succeeding in his plans.

Without a word, Tripp lifted me, setting me sideways on the saddle. Grabbing my thighs with rough hands. "I'll teach you anything you want, little doll."

I spread my legs wider and gripped his hand, tugging it under my dress. Directing him to my pussy with a brazenness I'd never displayed before. He groaned when he felt how wet my panties were, but I didn't stop there. No, I pushed the delicate pink lace aside and dragged his hand right up to my flesh. Working both our fingers against my clit. Keeping my eyes on his as I teased myself. As I got us started.

After a few strokes, I moved his hand down and slid his thick finger inside me with a sigh. "Teach me everything, Tripp. I want it all."

As I knew he would, my stallion took over. He plunged two fingers inside me, pressing his thumb against my clit and leaning over me until I was forced to arch my back and cling to his shoulders to keep from sliding off the leather seat of the saddle.

And then he started with the whispers.

"You like this? Knowing any of the other guys could come in here and see me with my fingers buried inside your cunt? Like knowing we've all been dreaming of getting up under this flirty little dress of yours and taking a piece of you? You do, don't you? Such a little dick tease, our doll."

He dropped down to plant a kiss on my lips, biting my bottom one until I gasped, then sliding his tongue inside. He tasted so good, all hot and minty and him. I wanted more. More of his tongue, of his taste. More of his fingers inside of me. Just *more*.

I grabbed his wrist, pulling him closer, deeper. He gave me what I needed, adding a third finger to the mix. Making me moan and shake as he stretched me. As he curled those fingers deep and hit a spot that had me seeing stars.

"Tripp," I gasped, every inch of me starting to tremble under his ministrations.

"That's it. Fuck, your pussy's so wet and hot already. You're going to be nice and swollen for me when I'm done, aren't you? Gonna be good and tight when I stuff you full of my thick cock. Can't wait to fill you up, doll. To come inside this little heaven and know my seed is dripping down your thighs. Make you walk past all the other guys, smelling of sex and me and leather. They'll be so fucking jealous. You're going to have six other men dying to bend you over one of these saddle racks."

A girl could dream.

My orgasm took me by surprise. One second, I was riding Tripp's hand, feeling the pressure build inside of me with every stroke and curl. The next, I was biting down on his shoulder as my world broke apart and put itself back together. As my body clenched down hard and time stood still before everything moved at the speed of light and set us back to rights. I was still coming, still clenching around his thick fingers, when Dalton ran into the room.

"Time to go back inside, princess." He froze, his eyes hot and hard as they took in our position. As they moved from my face down my flushed chest to where Tripp's hand disappeared under my skirt and between my legs. No way did he not know what we'd been doing, and no way did he not enjoy seeing us this way, if the bulge behind his fly was any indication.

But then his words sank in.

"What's wrong?"

He didn't answer me. "Tripp, now."

"Sorry, doll. Hang on to me." Tripp yanked his hand from inside of me and picked me up, throwing me over his shoulder like a sack of flour before running out the door. Dalton followed, Matthew joining him before we hit the big sliding doors that would lead us to the driveway.

We were inside the house in seconds, all four of us breathing hard. Me shaking like a leaf from the panic roaring through me. When Tripp finally set me on my feet, I got a good look at his face. Gone was the needy, sexy smile and lust-filled eyes. The man looked worried.

Tripp never looked worried.

"Calm down, doll."

As if. "In the history of the world, not one person has ever actually *calmed down* when someone's told them to. I'm not about to be the first. Tell me what's going on."

Dalton took that question as he moved to lock the back door.

"Quinn thinks we've got a visitor. Seems there's another camera looping, and it's attached to the outside of the barn."

The barn I'd just been inside, where my men had been working all day. So close. Too close. Quinn would hate himself for missing Chance's approach, for calling this downtime when we'd truly been under attack. "Is he okay?"

Dalton gave me a funny look, one filled with confusion. "Quinn? He's fine. We're all more worried about you right now." He nodded to Tripp. "You got her?"

"Yeah. I'm good."

Dalton and Matthew disappeared out the front while Tripp wrapped his body around mine and rocked me. Obviously trying to soothe my frazzled nerves. But there would be no soothing today—not until I had all seven of my men back under this roof.

Not until I figured out how to rid my herd of the threat against them.

Chapter Thirty-One

Four hours. It took my stallions four hours to secure the property, inspect all the cameras, install more to capture possible movement on all parts of the ranch, and feel safe enough to join Tripp and me inside. Matthew only popped his head in for a minute before rushing back out, taking on the job of patrolling while the rest of us had dinner. As soon as the men were done eating, Quinn and Garrett joined him, leaving me alone with Cade, Dalton, Liam, and Tripp.

Liam broke the post-meal silence first. "I know it's bad timing, Tripp, but I think it's a good idea if we have Waverley spend the night with Cade and Dalton."

I darted a glance at the two stallions in question—the men who did *everything* together. They appeared unaffected by Liam's words as if they'd already known this was coming.

"But it's Tripp's night with me," I said, the argument sounding weak even to my own ears.

Tripp leaned closer, looking unaffected and calm. "I've got some damn good memories to get me through the lonely night, doll. If the boss says you go with Cade and Dalton, then you go. You can always make it up to me next time you come to the barn for a visit. There are some lovely ropes we can play with out there."

Naughty boy. I gave him a weak smile, trying hard to stay positive. "I'll make it up to you anywhere you want."

The heat in his eyes flared, and he grabbed my hand. Tugging me out of my seat. "Come on. I'll help you grab your stuff."

I didn't have stuff. Not really, and definitely not in his room. I'd been given my own room in the house, though I didn't use it as anything more than a holding area for what little I'd brought with me when I'd run. Still, I followed Tripp down the hallway and into his room. Assuming he needed to talk to me.

I was so damn wrong.

As soon as he had the door closed, he grabbed me and lifted me up, up, up. Hooking my knees over his shoulders and pressing me against the wall. Almost knocking my head into the ceiling. Just like our first time together.

I wasn't naked this time, though, so he ripped my panties right off me, tossing the fabric to the side. And then his mouth was on my clit. Like earlier that morning, there was no teasing, no slow start or easy licks. Just abrupt, strong suction right on my bundle of nerves. The kind that sent shock waves straight to the heart of me. The kind that would make a girl come before she could even catch her breath.

I curled over him, crying out at the intensity of the attack, supporting myself with my hands on his shoulders as my body shuddered at his touch. As I let go of all my control and surrendered to whatever he had planned for me.

My orgasm came on hard and fast like a freight train, taking over my body in no time. Seconds. I came within seconds of him putting his mouth on me. Clenching on nothing and wishing, wanting, craving so much more. Needing his cock and his fingers, his filthy words and his big body covering mine. The weight of him on top of me as he drove his cock inside.

His mouth hadn't stopped working my pussy, but I missed him already. And by the way he clung to me, how he held me so tight, I assumed he felt the same way. This wasn't fair. Nothing about the situation was.

"Tripp." I ran a hand over his head, tugging lightly on his hair until he rested his head against my stomach. Needing his words more than anything. He didn't disappoint.

"That was just a teaser, doll. A little taste of what I had planned for you tonight." He let me drop down, keeping me pinned to the wall. Keeping his body covering mine and his hands gripping me tightly. "Goddammit, I want to tell Liam to fuck off and keep you here, but I can't. It's not safe for you."

"I'm sorry. It's your night, and I feel so bad—"

He kissed me, sliding his tongue between my lips to stop my words. Letting me taste myself on his lips as he took my mouth. As he slicked his tongue against mine in frenzied strokes. There was desperation in his kiss, fear and need and everything I already felt at the idea of not being with him tonight. Of missing out on time with him.

One night. That was all I'd wanted. But we would have to wait.

Tripp finally broke the kiss, breathing hard as he pressed his forehead to mine and held on to my ass. Clutching me to him as if trying hard not to let me go.

"You're going to have to walk out of here on your own, doll. I can't—"

His hands tightened, a groan rumbling through this chest. I wanted to cry. Wanted to throw a tantrum about missed opportunities and how unfair it was to cut his time with me short. But I couldn't... We both knew this was what was best, not just for me, but for the herd. And I would do anything for my stallions, even if that meant disappointing one. Temporarily.

"When all this madness is done," I said, cupping his cheek and forcing his eyes to mine. "When the threat is gone and we're back to normal, I'm going to spend that first weekend in your bed."

His lips tipped up, just barely, but enough for me to notice. "Yeah?"

"Definitely."

"I've got a better idea. How about we spend that first weekend out at the lake? We can go skinny-dipping."

"There's a lake on the ranch?"

"Out on the western edge of the property. It's nice and secluded out there."

"And we can spend a few days there?" I frowned, unable not to. "I'm not the biggest fan of tents. Or bugs. Or...camping."

"There's a cabin with indoor plumbing and everything."

"Sounds perfect." Grinning, I rose up to press a soft kiss to his lips, a goodbye one even if I refused to say the words. "I should get going."

"Yeah." He sighed, finally letting me go. Looking damn-near heartbroken. "Cade and Dalton live in the basement. It's super secure down there, which must be why Liam wants you with them. You'll be safe."

I nodded, accepting his words as true. That I'd be safe in the basement—that it was the best place for me. But as I walked down the hall and across the kitchen, as Cade led the way down the stairs with Dalton following behind me, I couldn't help but wonder.

Would my stallions be safe without me nearby?

Chapter Thirty-Two

The basement felt more like a fortress than the rest of the house—no windows broke the plain, dark walls, no obvious way out except the stairs I'd walked down. Trapped. I felt trapped down there. Add in the close proximity of Cade and Dalton—two of the most intimidating men I'd ever met—and my instinct to flee was on full alert.

These are my men. My mates. My stallions. They won't hurt me.

"So," I started, trying hard to pull up a smile for them. "What are we going to do to pass the time?"

The two shared a look—*they share everything*—before Cade said, "We'll be monitoring the security footage all night and watching the alarm board Quinn installed."

Well, there went the idea that maybe we could do something together so I could get to know them better. My fox felt pretty deflated at such a quick dismissal, and I wasn't far behind her. "Oh. Okay. I could just read, I guess."

Dalton grunted and stood from the small couch he'd been taking up room on, holding out a hand for me. "Want to watch with us?"

My answer was immediate, my smile way brighter than it had been since I'd walked downstairs. "Yes. I think I'd like that."

Two chairs and three bodies at the control panel meant I had to sit on someone's lap to watch the screens, but I didn't mind. Heck, I quite enjoyed it. Cade and Dalton were both big, strong, muscular men with rough hands and an even rougher demeanor. They intrigued me, but we had a job to do. A mission. We needed to watch for my ex-boyfriend Chance on the cameras and help keep the Hidden E and the herd safe.

It was almost a gift to feel so useful to my stallions.

"The lights here"—Dalton pointed to a large board of what looked like tiny Christmas tree lights held individually on a wooden board—"are for the various motion detectors and alarms we've installed around the farm. If anything moves or sets off one of these, a camera will turn on, and the others nearby will zero in on that area. If anyone steps foot on our property, we'll know."

It all seemed like so *much*. "But he's gotten on to the Hidden E twice, right? Did the alarms not work those times?"

Cade grunted. "They worked, but we didn't."

"What do you mean?"

Dalton answered my question. "The first time, we didn't have alarms out there for motion. He was able to loop the camera feed before we noticed he was there."

Right. All this was new...because of me. "You didn't need the cameras before."

Cade shook his head, his voice a deep rumble as he said, "We should have had them all along. If Liam had listened to me two years ago, we wouldn't have been caught with our pants down."

Heh. Pants down. As in naked. I should not be picturing them naked. So many days of being sexed up made my brain go into twelve-year-old-boy territory. Thankfully, neither man seemed to notice.

Dalton picked up where Cade had left off. "The second time the perp got on property to fuck with a camera is another thing altogether. We thought we were ready for anything, but the bastard made it all the way to the barn without setting off a single alarm. That's..."

He trailed off, shaking his head and staring hard at the monitors. All the camera feeds. All the little lights. So much in the way between the outside world and us.

I couldn't imagine how Chance was able to bypass it all. "It's impossible."

Dalton sighed and sat back, rubbing a hand over his close-cropped hair. "Not impossible because the bastard did it."

"Do you know how he got through the web?"

"The web?" Cade looked so confused by that—to the point that I almost felt bad for describing their elaborate set of motion detectors and alarms that way. The word seemed too simple for what they'd done.

"I...I just mean it seems very web-like. Like a spider web but not flat. All the cameras and motion detectors—they're not aimed at one point, right? So they form a sort of web of points to avoid." I looked from one man to the other, trying hard to find the right words to explain the image in my head. "Like that movie with that really hot actress—she's a thief and they go to steal something, but there are all these laser lines crisscrossing the room, so she has to twist and turn her body through them to get to the prize. It's super sexy and sensual but tactical at the same time. The contortion required to crawl through a web."

Cade's face went blank, his eyes burning into mine as he stared silently. I wanted so badly to fidget, to curl up against Dalton and seek his warmth, to escape from that penetrating stare, but I couldn't. Wouldn't. I refused to back down from one of my mates, even if he was making me incredibly uncomfortable.

Finally, he blinked and shot a glance to Dalton. "Get Quinn on the phone." Cade hopped up, pacing as Dalton moved me to the other chair and grabbed his phone. Calling Quinn instead of just walking upstairs. If my naughty professor was at his monitors, he might not hear the device go off.

"I could run up and get him," I offered, trying to be helpful.

Cade's growl made goose bumps appear on my arms. "Fuck no. You're not leaving the basement without one of us beside you. Preferably both of us."

I couldn't decide if I should be scared of the hulking shifter...or turned on by him. Something in the way he ordered me around, the way he demanded things, was so hot. Sort of like Matthew, but rougher. So much rougher. Easy to obey.

"Okay." My acquiescence came out as a whisper, barely more than breath over my lips. But Cade heard it. He stopped pacing and stared again, only moving closer when I shuddered from his hard glare.

"Are you afraid of me, woman?"

Woman. Why did I love being called that so much? "Yes. A little."

"I won't hurt you."

"I know that."

"Then why are you trembling?"

Honesty time. "Because I like your roughness. A lot."

His eyebrows flew up, and a slow smile curled his lips. "Do you want me to fuck you, Waverley?"

Oh. How could I not be honest with such a direct question? "Yes. Not this second because we have a job to do...but, yes. I want that."

"It's Tripp's night," Dalton said, coming up behind me and handing his phone to Cade. "Quinn's on the line."

Cade held my gaze for a little longer, looking almost ready to eat me for dinner. "You surprise me at every turn, fox." And then he was off, pacing again as he spoke into the phone. "I need a 3-D rendering of the security cameras and motion detectors. Sort of a trace of their viewpoints. Our little fox here said something about a web, and I think that might be our answer. We've been looking at everything in two dimensions instead of three."

For the next few hours, Cade and Quinn worked together on the various alarms and feeds, using their computers to manipulate the devices they could. Sending Matthew and Garrett out to manually adjust the ones they couldn't. I spent that time on Dalton's lap, warm and safe in his arms. Happy, too. I'd been helpful. I'd given my stallions another layer of security by thinking about webs and that hot actress's ass as she'd moved through those laser beams. It had been the highlight of the movie —unforgettable to see her twist and turn and bend all over the screen. Thank goodness for tight pants and great curves.

But even the excitement of the new security web couldn't keep me awake all night, and Dalton was just so warm and comfortable. I remembered listening to Cade and Quinn argue about a particular angle for a camera on the barn as I fought to keep my eyes open, and then there was a long stretch of nothing. I awoke suddenly, curled up in a chair alone, the lights on the alarm board glowing softly nearby. It took me a moment to get my bearings, to figure out where I was and what was going on. Cade and Dalton. The basement. They do everything together.

So, what were they doing?

A rhythmic sort of sound crept through the basement—nothing too loud or distinctive—but the addition of grunts and moans told me I'd see something naughty if I looked. Something the men might be doing on the other side of the room. Were they together? Solo? That moan sounded like Cade...not sure how I knew that, but I did. I could tell them apart by the simplest sounds, the way they stepped, the way their bodies moved. I knew the tone of that needy groan. I wanted to know what was happening, what had him sounding so pained and pleasured. What he could possibly be doing that had him grunting and smacking and... I quickly grew wet at the ideas running through my head. So very wet simply because of the sounds the men made, and I wanted to look. To see.

So I did.

I peeked under my arm, not wanting to move and give myself away. Feeling very much like Quinn with his voyeuristic tendencies. I told myself I'd take just a quick glance, but when I actually saw what was happening, I knew there was no way I could stop watching.

Cade.

With his very long, very hard, very pierced cock in his hand.

Stroking it.

His fist gripped his flesh in a steely grasp, nearly strangling it on every pull. That little bow tie of a piercing glittered in the light, subtle and small but obvious. At least to me...I'd been thinking about it since I saw it the first time. Been wondering what it would be like to touch it, kiss it, feel it inside me.

With every stroke up, the head of his dick grew darker, more filled with blood. And with every pull down, his one leg shook. Trembled. He was so ready to come.

And Dalton? He sat in a chair not five feet from Cade. Watching him. Pants off and one ankle crossed over his knee, cock in hand. Stroking all lazy and slow. The exact opposite of the way Cade was doing the same thing. As if he was savoring more than rushing, as if he enjoyed the tease more than the release. At least for the moment.

I watched and I grew hotter. Wetter between my legs. My skin flushed, and my nipples hardened almost painfully. I wanted to join them, to climb onto Dalton's lap and ride that hard cock until he couldn't stop from coming inside me. Wanted to take Cade in my mouth and flick my tongue against that little bow tie. I wanted both my stallions at once because they did everything together. But I couldn't move. Couldn't break up the scene across the room. I could only watch and want and crave.

I nearly slipped my hand between my legs when Cade sped up his movements, when he cursed and dropped his chin to his chest with a groan that almost made me come. When his hand flew over his cock, still gripping hard. And when he came, when he growled long and harsh, tilting his head back as thick white come wet his hand, I almost did too. So close. One touch of my clit, and I'd go off. I knew it, which was why I couldn't reach under my dress to tease myself. There was no way I could be silent.

Dalton rose from his seat, handing Cade a towel before grabbing him by the neck and pulling him in for a kiss. A strong, masculine, dangerous sort of kiss that looked almost painful and yet so completely them. *They do everything together*. I was so turned on by the brutality of the act, the roughness of it, that I didn't even think I'd need a single touch to get off. If they kept that up, I'd be coming with no manual stimulation whatsoever.

But even the best kisses must come to an end. The two men broke apart, whispering softly as they cleaned themselves up. As they moved back across the room. Toward me. I closed my eyes and pretended to still be asleep, not knowing how much they would have wanted me to see. If anything. That might have been a private moment—something I wasn't mean to see at all. Something just between them.

"She made me so hard." Dalton's voice reached me first, soft but clear. And obviously talking about me. "That ass in my lap all night about wrecked me, and the fact that she wasn't wearing panties definitely didn't help matters. I could feel her heat against my thigh all damn night. I was ready to slip inside her hours ago."

"Control, Dalton," Cade said, sounding much closer than I would have expected. Strong arms slipped underneath me suddenly, lifting me against a warm chest as the words continued rumbling through the quiet. "Liam's rules were clear—this should have been Tripp's night, so we can't have her. Tomorrow, she's ours."

He set me down on a bed, pulling a blanket over my shoulders as Dalton climbed in across from me. Cade's footsteps grew quieter—walking away—while Dalton wrapped me in his arms and pulled me close. Whispering against my hair as he cuddled me.

"A few more hours, princess. I know you're as hot as I've been all night, but we have to wait. Cade and I will fuck you good in just a few hours."

I gripped his arms, tugging him against me. Not caring that he knew I was awake...that I'd watched. Not caring about anything except his promise to *fuck me good* in a few hours.

I could hardly wait.

Chapter Thirty-Three

Hot. I woke up for the second time so darn hot. No wonder. Overnight, I'd become the meat in a stallion sandwich. I'd wrapped myself around Cade, my head resting on his chest and my legs tangled with his. Dalton lay at my back, pressing himself against me. Hanging on to my body as if afraid I might disappear. Not that there was any way to do that—not with a sexy stallion on either side of me.

But seriously, I was so hot. I shifted slightly, trying to determine how to extricate myself from their hold. Failing horribly at that task. But the room felt sweltering. I needed to escape.

Cade sighed and tugged me closer, making me even more uncomfortable. "Sleep, woman. While you can."

A hum sounded from behind me. "There's no rush this morning, princess. Get some more sleep."

Dalton's heavy hand rubbed along my hip, pulling me even closer. Letting me feel his morning wood. Reminding me that I was theirs today. All day. Yet I felt too hot and almost itchy to even think about those possibilities. I needed air.

"I'm going to take a shower," I said, patting Cade's arm until he rolled onto his back so I could crawl over him. Those ice-blue eyes met mine when I straddled him, my one leg reaching for the floor, the other lagging behind. My pussy landing square on that ridge. He was so damn hard and thick. Something I nearly whimpered about. But he looked tired, and I wanted to clean up before we did anything at all. So I kissed his cheek and whispered, "Sleep, my mate. You need to rest."

And then I hopped out of bed and headed for the bathroom at the far end of their room. I took one glance back at my men before heading inside, one peek before closing myself off from them. They both had stayed in bed, not snuggling really, but connected. Bodies touching. So comfortable already, so familiar with one another. I had no idea how I was going to fit into their relationship.

A thought I brushed away almost before it had even finished swirling through my mind.

They wanted me, wanted to share me between them. I may not have had multiple partners at once before, but I would figure it out. They'd teach me.

I couldn't wait for them to start teaching me.

The warm water raining down on me did a lot to clear my head and wake me up, though it also caused the heat building inside of me to burn brighter. I turned the temperature lower. And again. And again until I stood under a cold spray of water. No matter how cool the water was, my body felt too hot, my skin too tight. I needed something, and a shower wasn't it. This heat came from somewhere inside of me, somewhere deep within my instincts and needs. This heat was practically a force of nature.

I needed my men. My stallions. I needed to get off and to get them off, needed to feel them inside of me, on top of me, all over me. I needed to be surrounded by their scent and their skin, to wear nothing but their breaths and their words. I needed all of it.

And that was how I knew I'd gone into a mating heat cycle.

My fox paced in my mind, too worked up to sit still. Wanting to get outside and run. To force her mates to chase her through the woods then let them catch her and pin her down. Fox shifters didn't go into heat as often as some of the other breeds, but I'd been through this a few times. I knew what was coming and what would satisfy the ache that would only be growing stronger.

Thankfully, I had seven big, strong mates to help me through the next couple of days. Heck, if Cade and Dalton had been awake, they probably would have smelled the heat on me already. They would have known how much I needed them to pleasure me. But I wanted them to sleep, so I was alone. Without a single toy in sight. In a shower but without a removable shower head. Definitely not a single woman's bathroom.

Unable to stop myself, I slipped a hand between my legs and ran my fingers over my clit. Sparks shot up my abdomen and spine, making me shiver. Making me gasp quietly. I could do this—I liked my toys and things, but I'd made myself orgasm with just my hand before. And then, once I came and gave myself a little breathing room, I could hunt down my men. It was Cade and Dalton's day, after all. They'd care for me. I just needed to take the edge off so I didn't attack them as soon as I walked out of the bathroom.

I was leaning against the wall of the shower—one hand against my mouth to keep from calling out and the other buried between my legs, three fingers deep inside myself—when the shower door suddenly opened.

"Would you look at this?" Dalton said, eyeing me. Looking so damn rough and male and sexy. "Our princess needed our cocks but was too shy to say anything. Is that what's going on here?"

Cade pushed past him, grabbing my arm and tugging it from between my legs as he towered over me. "It's our day."

But I'd been so close. "I...it's just—"

"You think we don't know you've gone into heat, woman?" Cade leaned over me, licking up the length of my wet fingers and growling. "We could smell you from the bed. You're in need, and we've come to satisfy you."

Oh my. I melted into him, darting a look to Dalton. Holding one and watching another. Cade—my big, strong soldier of a man—took complete control, pinning me to the wall and shoving his roughened hand against my pussy. Making me call out and quake as he attacked my clit.

"She's good and wet, D. I think she's ready for us."

I was. I *so* was. But before I could answer, Cade pulled me from the wall and shoved me backward, forcing me against Dalton's hard chest. The water rained down on all of us, cooler than it needed to be and yet adding to the moment. Making everything seem more intimate, more secret. As if the shower would cover all the dirty words that wanted to spill from my lips and hide the fact that I stood naked with two men.

Dalton grabbed my breast from behind me, squeezing nice and tight as he rocked his hard dick against my ass. "You ready for me, princess? Is that pussy wet enough for me to slide this big cock inside?" He bent over me, dropping a kiss along my jaw before whispering, "You're going to have both of us on you. All over you. Eventually, you'll have both of us inside you. I bet my little fox loves that idea. Two big stallions fucking your greedy holes as you bliss out between them. I bet you want us to use you so hard."

Oh hell.

"Yes," I gasped, spreading my legs wider as he directed his cock between my thighs. "I want that. So much."

"We'll get there," Cade said, dropping to his knees before me. "Right now, you need to come. Why were you suffering alone when you could have ridden any one of your herd's cocks?"

I could barely think, let alone remember, But I did because my mate wanted me to. Was waiting on my answer. "It's your day—you and Dalton—but I wanted to let you sleep."

Cade looked up at me, his ice-blue eyes piercing, before flicking a glance over my shoulder. His hands gripped my thighs tight as he growled, "If you need to be fucked, you wake me up. Understand?"

I nodded, unable to speak as Dalton slid his heavy cock inside of me. That had been the glance over my shoulder—Cade's way of telling Dalton to go. And Dalton followed that unspoken direction, moving slow, so very slow. I closed my eyes and bent over slightly, giving him room. Wanting more of him. Wanting hard and fast and balls deep. But he took his time, teasing me as he rocked himself in and out, in and out, sliding deeper every time. Not nearly deep enough.

"Our girl needs more," Cade said as he spread two fingers and dragged them over my entrance, teasing me and Dalton at the same time. "This isn't the time to be playful, D."

"Got it." Dalton grunted and slammed home, almost knocking me off my feet as he filled me with his cock. And my god was it glorious. The stretch, the power of his thrust—I could have come right then. Could have screamed his name and clenched around him, milking his cock with my pussy. But I didn't because Cade—that filthy fucking stallion— maneuvered himself between my thighs and clamped his lips around my clit. As Dalton pounded into me from behind, Cade suckled me to the point of pain. To the point of bare, unfiltered need.

To the point that I was coming all over Dalton's dick in less time than I could have possibly imagined.

Neither man stopped, though. They didn't give me a break from the sensations at all, at least not until Dalton came with a full-body shudder and a growl worthy of any predator shifter.

As Dalton eased back, Cade rose to his feet, grabbing me by the hips and flipping me around. Pushing me into a slight bend as he directed his cock into me. Rough and fast and totally in control. Not at all gentle. I loved it. I also loved the twinge from the metal barbell embedded in his flesh. A totally new sensation and one that I hoped to experience again. Slower. At a time when I could savor the feeling of it.

Now was not that time.

"You want more, woman? Suck him. Bend over and wrap those dick-tease lips around his cock." Cade grunted and fucked into me harder, one hand dropping down to tease my clit. And Dalton? He looked desperate for me—already heated and wanting, even though he'd just come. The scent of my heat filled the steamy space, likely adding to his impressive recovery. Males went insane over females in heat in the fox world— chased their mates down and fucked them until they could barely move. All because of that warm, luscious scent. My stallions didn't seem immune to it either.

"Waverley," Dalton said, gritting his teeth. Looking just as wild and out of control as I felt. I knew what he wanted, what he needed. So as Cade tortured my pussy with his hand and his cock, I did what I'd been told to do. Bent at the waist and took Dalton right into my mouth. He tasted like me—like us—something that had me moaning and sucking harder, wanting to get to just him. Wanting to take him into my throat and taste his come on my tongue.

"Fuck, princess. Your mouth is so damn hot." Dalton grabbed my shoulders and pushed deeper, fucking my mouth slowly. Not pushing too hard or too fast as we both got used to the size and depth. Cade had slowed down as well, giving us time to adjust, though he kept that bastard finger against my clit, kept flicking over my bundle of nerves and making me shake while his cock sat buried inside of me.

I wasn't in the mood to be a passive lover, though.

Grabbing Dalton by the hips, I yanked him closer. Bringing him deep inside my mouth. I rolled my hips against Cade at the same time, trying to make him move. To take him deeper, to fuck him instead of the other way around. He seemed to take the hint, pounding into me nice and hard, grunting as his balls slapped against my ass and his fingers pinched my clit.

"She's a little cock slut," Cade said, groaning loudly as I clenched my pussy around his length. "Fuck me, our woman likes the dick. You like getting fucked, Waverley? Because you're in the right place if you do. Dalton and I have two big dicks for you to take—your pussy, your mouth, your ass. Whatever you want."

"Not gonna last." Dalton grabbed my head and held me in place as he rocked his hips, as he fucked my face. Taking from me and not giving me a break for a single second. And I loved it. "Fucking mouth is too good. So hot and wet. Almost as good as that sweet pussy."

"Sweet is right. You should get a taste of her next time. She was sweet as sugar dripping down my chin." Cade ground deep, pressing hard on my clit. "Tug on his balls, woman. He likes that. He'll come all down your throat if you give him a good pull."

I did as directed, grabbing Dalton by the balls and tugging. Harder than I normally would have, but I was out of control at that point. So close to coming, I couldn't see straight. So filled from both ends, I couldn't do anything but feel and do whatever my stallions wanted me to.

Dalton came on the first tug, cursing a blue streak as he released inside my mouth. I swallowed every drop, licking over the tip of him before releasing his cock. And Cade—he just kept pounding into me. Fucking me hard. So hard. At least until Dalton added his hand between my legs, pressing up on my clit as he forced me to stand straight again. Leaning closer so he could pin me against Cade.

"His dick's good, isn't it?" Dalton said, rolling the heel of his hand against my clit. "Clench hard on him, princess. He likes that. Clench nice and strong, and he'll come inside you. Fill you up with all his come and satisfy your heat for now."

Oh yes. Yes, yes, yes. I clenched hard, tightening my muscles and dropping my head back against Cade's shoulder. Looking up at him as I whispered, "I want your come inside me. I need it."

Cade groaned and shook, coming with a hard expression on his face and a deep thrust that filled me to the point of pain. I responded with a strong aftershock, my pussy quivering all over his cock. Sucking him deeper. Claiming every drop of his release.

Strangling him as he practically broke me in two.

"Goddamn," Cade said, dragging his teeth over my neck as he pulled out of me. "Best fucking pussy in the world and made just for us."

Yes, I was. I totally was. And they were all made just for me.

My men cleaned me up carefully, lovingly rubbing a towel over my sensitive flesh and dropping soft kisses all over my body. They chuckled when I sagged into their arms, mocking my exhaustion. I couldn't help it, though. The heat had abated, but I was tired. So very tired. My body and my brain needed a long nap to process everything and recover from such an intense experience.

Thankfully, Cade and Dalton were more than ready to put me to bed. But when we stepped out of the bathroom, we weren't alone. Liam stood at the bottom of the stairs, and he looked positively livid.

"Everyone upstairs. Now."

Chapter Thirty-Four

Breakfast should have been a nice, calm affair, what with Dalton feeding me as I sat on Cade's lap with all my men around me. Sadly, that wasn't the case.

"The bastard tried four times to breach the barn, but we were able to stop him. We just couldn't actually catch him." Liam huffed, his shoulders stiff and a heavy scowl on his handsome face. Pissed off. My ex was driving my stallions crazy, and there wasn't much I could do about it.

"He's close," Matthew said, looking just as upset as Liam. "He's so close, I can smell the fucker. One mistake, and he's going down. I was right behind him last night, but he slipped away from me. If I could have just—"

"We stick to the plan," Liam said, his voice a deep rumble as he shot a glare at the dominant stallion. "We do not engage without another member of the herd for backup."

"Liam's right," Cade said, his face hard and his gaze strong. "Only Dalton and I have the training to take this guy on alone. He's human, but he's got skills. Do not underestimate him."

The bad boy of the herd scoffed. "Fucker's got nothing on us."

"No, he doesn't," Liam said, growling through his words. "And we're going to keep it that way. He's close—almost close enough to make a play. When he does, I want a team ready to take him out. Not a lone man who might not be able to make this a clean capture."

Matthew didn't look happy about that one bit. In fact, he kicked his chair back and stood up from the table in a huff. "We're finishing this today. Let's go, Garrett."

The two headed out the door, Matthew looking fiercely angry as he slammed out the screen door. Garrett at least stopped to kiss the top of my head and rub my shoulder on his way out. Something Matthew had neglected to do. I appreciated the kindness, though I also understood Matthew's frustrations. This was wearing on all of us.

Liam sat back in his chair, staring up at the ceiling as if the white surface might give him some sort of direction. Looking very much like a lost man needing something to find him. Something...or someone. I patted Cade's thigh and slipped off his lap, heading for our leader. Wanting to do anything I could to ease his strain.

"Hey there. You smell so damn good," Liam said as I straddled his lap and kissed his neck. He likely meant the scent of my heat, which had been increasing again since we'd come upstairs. But that wasn't why I was on him.

"You've hardly eaten."

He sighed. "Too distracted to eat."

"Should I make you a cake? Something sweet to tempt you with?" I sat back, grinning. Almost vibrating with excitement when his lips quirked up in a half smile.

"If I wanted something sweet, I'd just eat you, sugar."

Yeah, he would. He loved the taste of me—or so he'd said. But today was about Cade and Dalton, and Liam had a job to do. So with a big, smacking kiss and a pat on my ass, he helped me to my feet.

"Quinn's on cameras for two more hours," Liam said, looking right at Cade. "Pretty sure every man in this room knows what's going on with our girl right now, so I want you two focused on her. Whatever she needs, she gets."

"Not a problem," Dalton replied, yanking me down onto his lap and sliding his hand between my legs. "I was just thinking it was time to head back to the safety of the basement for a while."

Where we could be alone. Where they could ease the burning inside of me. "Yeah. Okay. Let's do that."

I didn't even blush as the men laughed at my eagerness. Instead, I led the way downstairs, leaving Tripp to clean up the breakfast dishes on his own. He didn't seem to mind—in fact, he'd shot me a wink and an air kiss before turning for the sink. They all knew I was in a needful way. Next time, it might be their turn to take care of me through the mating fever. To use their bodies to sate the fire within.

I was almost across the basement room when strong hands grabbed me around the waist, and then I was flying. I landed in a heap on the bed, rolling to the head of it with a laugh. "What was that for?"

Cade, the perpetrator of the toss, tugged his shirt over his head, looking like a man on a mission. "Your heat is building. You need to be fucked."

Blunt much? "I'm fine if there's something else—"

Dalton rolled onto the mattress beside me, already shirtless and with his pants unfastened. His hands zeroed in on my hips to yank me toward him. "Fine isn't good enough, princess. We want you satisfied. Are you satisfied yet?"

No. In fact, the more they talked and undressed and looked at me as if I was their greatest desire, the worse I felt. The hotter I burned. The more I needed. "No. I'm not satisfied yet."

Cade grunted. "Take care of her, D."

"What about you?" I asked, frowning at my seventh mate. "I can handle both of you."

Cade's smile turned absolutely wicked. "You're not quite ready for both at once, woman. Soon, though. Matthew may have started the work, but two at once isn't the same as being fucked while wearing a plug. Besides, right now, I just want to watch."

Like Quinn. Oh my stars, that was hot.

Dalton started nice and slow, sliding my shirt—Cade's shirt, really— up to my neck then sucking my nipple into his mouth with a groan. Cade settled on the chair next to the bed, turning it so he could get a good view. Sitting deep, spreading his legs and immediately taking his cock in his hand.

He didn't stay silent, though. "Don't look at me, woman. Dalton's the one who's going to make that pussy nice and wet."

"While you watch."

"Yeah."

"Like Quinn."

Cade cocked his head, darting his eyes down to Dalton, who was settling between my thighs.

"Go ahead," Dalton said, as if his partner had already asked him a question. "I've got some serious eating to do if I'm going to make this little lady scream for me."

And oh, he meant it. His tongue hit my clit, making me fall back. Sending shock waves throughout my body. Still, I stared at Cade. Mesmerized by his hand gripping his hard cock. Remembering how he'd sat and watched Dalton jack off the night before. How he'd fucked me so hard and well in the shower that morning.

Realizing how little I knew about them.

"How did you two meet?" Talking wasn't easy—not with Dalton licking and sucking on the flesh between my legs—but I did it. I arched my back and closed my eyes for a second as Dalton's tongue swept right over my clit in a lashing motion, but I kept my focus. Looked at Cade and watched as he flicked that little metal bow tie in his cock. The one I had yet to play with.

Cade seemed surprised by that question. "We grew up in the same herd."

Dalton hummed his agreement before backing away from my flesh and sliding two fingers inside me. "He was a bully in the pasture."

I closed my eyes for another second and groaned, focusing on the pleasure of being filled by him. Reaching down to grab his wrist when it wasn't enough. "More. Please."

Dalton chuckled and circled my clit with his thumb. "Only because you asked so nicely."

Once he had me whining and twisting for more, he pulled his hand from my body and rolled me over, lying on his back to position me on top of his hips. Hanging on as I slowly sank down on his thick, hard cock. "Better, princess?"

I could only nod because *better* didn't begin to describe how good he felt as he slid deeper and deeper. Besides, I needed my words for other things. "You two remind me of military men."

"Because we are," Cade said, going back to stroking his cock as he watched me bounce on Dalton's. "D and I spent a number of years in the Marines before all the medical tests and computers made it too hard to hide our true nature."

Marines. No wonder they were so tough and mean. So rough around the edges.

Dalton surprised me with a big thrust up, nearly knocking me off-balance and hitting something delicious inside of me. "What else, Waverley? What do you want to know about us? Keep bouncing on my cock, and we'll tell you everything."

Oh, but I couldn't think. He was so deep inside of me. The way he held my hips and ground against me did delicious things to my clit. I trembled and hissed, moving faster. Needing more. Wanting to hit that peak with him. And still, I watched Cade as he rose to his feet and moved closer. I tried hard to think, to find something to say, the right formation of letters to ask him what he was doing or where he was going. Words were so hard, though. Too hard.

"Ask him," Cade said as he slipped in behind me, leaning his big body into mine and holding on to my hips. "Ask him something, and I'll give you a treat."

I clutched his arm, still bouncing on Dalton, still so close to coming, I could almost taste it. Fighting my desire to let go to follow Cade's instructions. To get my treat. "How did you know?"

"Know what? Be specific." Cade bent my body over a little, dragging his hand up my spine.

"That you...together. That the two of you..."

"Were bisexual?"

I shivered, fantasizing about them together like *that*. About watching them. I was going to come just thinking about such things. "Yes. Yes, that."

"We just did. It was always us, you know? We were best friends growing up, but when we hit puberty, we both knew we needed more. Being together was as natural as breathing, but we've always wanted a woman with us as well. Our herd kicked us out after they found out about us, but Liam and Matthew took us right in and never said a word about it. Just gave us our space to be who we were as we all waited for our fated mate."

I couldn't even imagine being shunned by my skulk, my family, for nothing more than the way I loved. Couldn't think about it. I focused instead on the men of the Hidden E and how they'd created a family so easily. "That's beautiful."

"It is. And now we have you, which finally makes us all complete." Cade gripped me tighter, his voice slipping deeper as he said, "Are you ready for your treat?"

A pop sounded in the room, pleasure exploding through my pussy. He'd smacked me square on the ass, hard and quick. Making my skin burn and my pussy quiver, making Dalton groan long and loud as I clenched around him. I fell forward, bouncing harder. Keening as Dalton fucked me deep and Cade grabbed my ass with both hands.

"You like that, woman? Like to be treated like a naughty girl? How'd you like it if I spanked you while I fucked your ass? Would that make you feel better? Make your heat die down?"

I couldn't speak, couldn't think of words because something cold and wet was coating my asshole and Cade was rising up behind me. The only thing I could even think of to say was *yes* and *please* and *please* again.

"No need to beg," Dalton said, slowing down and peeking over my shoulder. "Cade's got you, princess. We'll make sure this first time is so good for you."

"Absolutely." Cade's thick finger slid into my ass, making me clutch at Dalton as the two filled me. As they worked in tandem to bring me to the brink. But then Cade retreated, only to come back a minute later.

"Push back for me," he said as something bigger and thicker slid between my cheeks. As it pushed inside. His cock. Double penetration. One in my pussy, one in my ass, surrounded by my stallions as my body burned for both of them. A total fantasy and a dream come true. The sting didn't matter, the pressure building didn't matter. Nothing mattered but the fire building inside of me and the feel of my men surrounding me.

"Yes, yes. Fill me up. Please. I need it."

"Fuck, she's so hot." Cade rocked and pushed deeper, moving slowly as Dalton held still beneath me.

"She's tight, too. Jesus, fuck—she's so tight on my cock." Dalton grabbed me by the shoulders and pulled me flat against his chest, kissing me deeply. Both of us groaning loudly as Cade seated himself in my ass.

"There we go," Cade said before sliding back a few inches. "Stuffed to the limits, aren't you? Fuck, you're so damn tight. I'm going to blow quick like some sort of teenager here. Make her come, D. I can't wait."

Dalton fucked up harder, both men working back and forth and driving me to the brink. Grunting and groaning and writhing against me. Dalton kept his hand on my clit, too—rubbing and circling and pressing as Cade whispered the filthiest words in my ear.

"You're going to feel me for days, woman. You'll be dripping our come down your thighs too. Every stallion here will know I took your ass today. They'll be so damned jealous that I filled you up with my come back here while Dalton filled that greedy pussy. They'll all be begging to get inside this sweet heaven."

I dropped my head to Dalton's chest, groaning as my pleasure spiked, as it grew and pulsed...as it broke. As my body locked down on both cocks and sent the three of us into a writhing, moaning mass of humanity.

There was no denying I'd had two men when all was said and done—my ass stung and the wet spot beneath us was...well, twice as big as normal. But when Cade picked me up and carried me to the shower, and when Dalton stood behind me and washed my hair as he whispered how perfect I was for them and how happy they were that I was there, none of that mattered.

I was with my stallions, and for one brief moment, nothing outside of that room could touch me.

Chapter Thirty-Five

The day was spent in both heaven and hell. I had two of my stallions to tease me, to make me come over and over whenever my heat built up. That was the heaven. The hell was that we also had to keep an eye on the security feed for most of the afternoon and evening. I didn't mind doing it, but my men became much more intense when they were watching the screens, more aggressive. And me? I became obsessed with the waiting. No way was Chance leaving me alone. He was out there, in the dark on the farm with most of my herd of stallions. Trying hard to break through our safety net. And he was dangerous.

"Here." Cade set a plate in front of me, making me turn away from the camera monitors. It was...

"Chicken and cookies?" I looked up at him, noticing his tight expression and furrowed brow. The way he seemed almost uncomfortable.

"Yeah, well...you need protein, and foxes like sweets."

Aw, my big soldier was trying to be nice. "We do, especially me. Cookies are my favorite. This is the perfect dinner for me, especially after a day in your bed. Thank you."

A smile crept across his face, but it was fleeting—the monitors caught his attention, and he went right back to frowning. "We good out there?"

"All's quiet." Dalton rose to his feet and stretched, groaning. "Liam wants me to take over patrolling for Garrett and Matthew."

"Solo?" Cade asked, looking all sorts of unhappy about that.

"Sounds like it."

"You planning on carrying?"

I looked from Cade to Dalton, unsure what Cade meant. Dalton nodded and opened a metal cabinet. He pulled out a leather contraption and slipped it on over his shoulders. Buckles were fastened, and then he—

He pulled out a gun.

"Sweet mercy," I whispered, unable not to. Unable to think about one of my men needing a weapon.

"It's just as a precaution, princess," Dalton said, hurrying over once his gun was secured under his arm to grab my face and drop soft kisses on my lips. "No one's getting close to you."

I grabbed his arms, holding him in place. "What if they get close to you?"

Cade just chuckled. "We hope this fucker does."

I didn't. But my men were strong, and Dalton had been a Marine. He knew what he was doing. Still...

"Come back to me," I said before letting Dalton go.

He took a few steps back, beaming as he headed for the stairs. "Anything for you, princess. Anything at all."

And then he was gone, his footsteps pounding up the stairs. Leaving me alone with—

"Eat," Cade said with no real force behind his words. He looked as upset as I did, just in his own way. He had to be as worried as I was— likely more considering how long he and Dalton had been together.

"He'll be okay." I wasn't sure whether I was trying to convince him or me. My words didn't seem to work on either of us, though.

"He'd goddamned well better be."

And so we went back to what we'd been doing—staring at the images and video from outside. Cade fed me a few pieces of chicken and I nibbled on a cookie, but I couldn't really eat. My stomach was in knots as I worried about my stallions. All of them.

"C'mere, Waverley."

I looked up to find Cade sitting with his arms open, waiting for me. Probably needing my comfort as much as I needed his. I didn't hesitate. I hopped right over onto his lap and curled up against his chest. Sighing as his warmth enveloped me. "I wish this were over."

"Soon, my woman. It'll be over soon. We're frustrating this human, which is a good thing. He'll try something more direct, and then we'll have him. Tonight, more than likely."

I hoped he was right.

Hours passed that way—me on Cade's lap, both of us staring at camera feeds from across the farm. I saw each of my men on those screens as the hours passed—knew they were alive and okay, at least for a fleeting moment, as the night wore on. Those glimpses gave me hope, soothed me for the briefest of instants before I lost sight of my stallions again.

After an immeasurable amount of time, Cade groaned and shifted beneath me. "Your heat is growing stronger again."

I shrugged, too tired to care. Too worried to bother. "It's fine."

Cade dropped a hand high up on my thigh and squeezed, his fingers practically teasing my pussy. "If it becomes not fine, let me know. I can multitask to keep you comfortable. Or we can call one of the guys back here to take over in front of the video board while I sate your needs."

Those words pulled the first smile from me in hours. So considerate, this man. "Thanks. I appreciate it."

He kissed the top of my head, a sweet move that warmed me more than my heat did. "You're our girl. We take care of you."

Yeah, they did. All of them. To their detriment, it seemed.

Suddenly, something flashed on one of the screens. A shape—one I knew well—racing across the back of the barn. "Cade...it's Matthew."

Cade stiffened, leaning closer to the screen in question. It was definitely Matthew, and he was running fast, his image almost blurring as it moved from screen to screen.

Cade pressed a button on the control panel and leaned close to the microphone sitting on the counter. "Back of the barn, heading for the driveway. I've got Matthew in a full sprint."

"Fuck." That sounded like Liam's voice coming through the speakers. "I'm on my way."

"Too far," Dalton said, his voice staticky. "I'm closer. You got eyes on what he's running toward?"

"Negative." Cade adjusted the screens, moving the feeds to try to get a better view in front of Matthew. "Come on, fucker. Show yourself."

I watched as Matthew shifted on the fly, as his big, beautiful horse appeared almost out of nowhere and galloped for the front of the barn. My heart pounded, and I could barely breathe, knowing this was it. Chance was definitely on Hidden E property, and Matthew was chasing him...on his own. He'd ignored Liam's and Cade's directives to stay with a partner, not to go out alone, and the backup he needed didn't appear to be nearby.

This could be trouble.

"Who's closest?" I asked, looking at every screen and trying to judge where every stallion was, my heart racing harder with every second that passed. Too long. Everything was suddenly taking too long. "Damn it, Matthew needs help. Who can get to him?"

"I'm closest," Cade said as he hopped to his feet, nearly knocking me over. "You stay here."

Oh, hell no. I would *not* be left behind when my stallions—my mates —needed me. I was about to chase after Cade, who'd already run up the stairs, when a low rumble caught my attention. The sound of an engine. Coming from the security feed.

I stared at the screens in confusion as some sort of light lit up one screen.

As Matthew in horse form veered and seemed to slip on the gravel drive.

As a large tractor—the one the guys used to haul hay into the barn from the back pastures—shot forward from its lean-to.

I stood there helpless, watching as the tractor slammed into my Matthew. As my dominant mate seemed to bend almost in half in a way his big equine body wasn't mean to and went flying offscreen.

As my world came to a crashing halt.
"No."

Chapter Thirty-Six

It took me far too long to make my way up the stairs and out of the kitchen. It seemed to take even longer to run across the driveway to where Matthew—still in his stallion form—lay still and quiet. Every movement taking three times as long as it should have. Every sound muddled as if I were somehow under water. And all the while, I stared. Transfixed by the black beast sprawled across the dirt. Wishing and praying to every deity known to man that he'd move. That he'd show me just one sign of life.

My prayers were answered with a simple flick of a tail.

"Matthew." I dropped to my knees beside him, one hand on his shoulder as I leaned over and buried my face in his mane. "Please be okay. Please. I can't lose you. I can't lose any of you."

"Waverley." Tripp settled in beside me, covering my hand with his and wrapping one big, strong arm around my shoulders. "He'll be okay. He just needs a few minutes to heal."

Because he was a shifter, and shifters were hard to kill. I knew this. I *knew* it, and yet...seeing him flying through the air had broken something inside of me. Days of fear and worry and stress had built up too high for me to hold back, and watching Matthew go down had toppled the tower. I wasn't just worried anymore. I was angry.

Scratch that—I was fucking furious.

"You've got him?" I asked, my words harsh but flat. The heat inside me no longer based on lust but rage.

Tripp released my hand, moving his to check over Matthew's muscled chest. "I do. I won't let anything happen to him."

Good. "Where is he?"

Liam walked up beside us, not seeming to need me to explain the *he* I meant. "Cade has him."

"I want to see him."

"I don't think that's a good idea."

"I don't care what you think right now." I gave Matthew a kiss to his muzzle then rose to my feet, ignoring the stallion trying to stop me. Liam may have been the leader of the herd, but he wasn't about to tell me what to do—not tonight. "Cade! Cade, get out here."

Cade and Dalton appeared out of the shadows, both holding on to a very surly-looking Chance. Surly, filthy, and slightly bloody. They must have gotten a few hits in as they caught him. Good.

"You." I pointed at the human in our midst, letting every ounce of my rage explode out of me. "You don't deserve to breathe the same air as these men do."

"This is what you left me for? These...freaks?" Chance spat on the ground, making a big production out of the move. "I've seen them change into horses. You think their unnaturalness is going to scare me off? Not happening, sweetheart. No messed-up human-horse hybrids are going to stop me from taking what's mine."

Oh, hell no. "I'm not yours. I never have been."

"You're wrong, but I'll remind you as soon as I get you away from here."

"I'm not going anywhere with you. Liam?"

My first stallion lover, the leader of our family herd, placed a hand on my shoulder. "Yes, sugar?"

I kept my eyes on Chance's, kept my face as flat and emotionless as I could. Kept my mind focused on what was best for my herd. "I want him gone."

Chance laughed. "Go ahead and call the cops—have me arrested. I'll come back for you, Waverley. I'll always come back for you."

He would, too. I knew it—my stallions knew it—which meant calling the cops was out of the question. We would have to handle things quietly and keep what happened on the Hidden E. And only on the Hidden E.

"I never said anything about the cops. That's human law." I took a step closer, fighting Liam's hold on me. Needing to make one last point. "Human law might claim we're the ones doing something wrong, but in shifter law, threatening a fated mate is a crime punishable by death. You're on shifter property, and so you'll follow our rules. You don't get to leave this place. Not ever. My men here, my *herd*, will make sure of that."

"You heard the lady," Liam said, tugging me into his side as he lifted a chin at Cade and Dalton. "Get rid of the problem, but let me know if you need any help. I wouldn't mind tearing into a piece of him."

"We've got this," Cade said, looking downright terrifying as he glared down at Chance.

Chance's eyes grew wide, the realization of the situation he'd found himself in seeming to wash over him. "You won't get away with this. Everyone knew Waverley and I were meant to be together. They all talked about how perfect we were for each other. If I go missing, the cops will come looking for her."

I shrugged. "They won't find me, and even if they do, they won't find you."

Chance continued blathering and hollering as Cade and Dalton dragged him off into the night. I didn't care what he had to say, though. All of my worry centered on Matthew. On making sure my entire herd was safe.

I turned my back on my past without a second thought to his fate. He'd earned whatever was about to happen to him. "How's Matthew?"

Tripp looked up at me, smiling. "He's fine, doll. Another minute and he'll shift back to his human self and be the cranky old Dom you know and love."

One could only hope.

It took longer than a minute, and the shift looked more painful than any I'd ever seen, but eventually, an exhausted-looking Matthew lay naked and panting in the dirt.

"How you doing, man?" Tripp asked, helping Matthew sit up.

"I feel like I was hit by a truck." Matthew groaned, clinging to Tripp's arm as he weaved a little. "Did I get him?"

I had to laugh at that one. My one-track-mind mate. "Yeah. You got him, you silly beast. Why didn't you wait for the others?"

"I had to keep you safe." Matthew looked up at me, a cut over his eyebrow dripping blood down his face. I wiped away the worst of it, holding his gaze. Inching closer to my brave, stupid mate.

Matthew grabbed my hand, flicking an irritated glance at the blood covering my thumb and forefinger. "That's going to leave a mark, isn't it?"

"Probably. Don't worry, though—scars are hot."

His lips turned up in the smallest, weakest grin I'd ever seen. Not that I was complaining.

"Yeah? Then I'll have to acquire a few more. Anything to get you back into my bed."

I leaned over to kiss just above the cut on his forehead. "Let's keep the scars to a minimum. You don't need them to get me into your bed— I'm a sure thing."

"See? I knew you were our perfect mate." He smiled, looking stronger with every second that passed. "You okay now, bunny?"

Silly stallion. "Why are you asking me that?" I said, cupping his face in my hands. "You're the one who got hit by a tractor."

Matthew grabbed me by the wrists, tugging me closer. "If you let me get inside that tight ass again, it'll have been worth it."

"Pretty sure it's still Cade and Dalton's night," Liam said as he helped Matthew to his feet. Matthew wobbled a bit, but Tripp and Liam held him up. Helped him to the porch and inside the house, while Garrett and Quinn followed behind us. My herd mostly complete.

"I think they'll understand that Matthew needs to be nursed back to health," I said as the boys settled in at the kitchen table.

"Do you have a naughty nurse outfit?" Matthew asked, still looking too pale and obviously hurting. "Because I could go for that."

"Right now, I think you need to go for some pain pills and sleep."

He frowned. "Damn."

We waited around for Cade and Dalton to join us, joking and laughing to help the time pass. No one mentioning what we all knew was going on outside. Every one of us completely focused on keeping Matthew as comfortable as we could. And when the last two stallions in our herd came stomping into the kitchen, looking even darker and wilder than they usually did, I knew things were done.

Chance was dead.

Our herd was finally safe.

"She's all ours, boys," Cade said, leaning a shoulder against the wall and giving me one hell of a sexy smirk. "Whatever should we do with her?"

I grinned, unable not to run to him. To wrap myself around him and whisper my thanks into his neck. Dalton cuddled in close too, both of them holding on to me. Soon enough, I had seven men in a group hug, all trying to touch me, to hang on to our connection. To feel. And I loved every single one of them.

"You're all mine," I said, unable not to shed a tear. "I get to keep you all."

"Yeah, you do, sugar," Liam said. "And more importantly, we get to keep you."

They did. They really, really did.

Epilogue

Pregnancy agreed with me.

Tripp handed me another glass of sweet tea—decaffeinated because of the baby—and settled in behind me. Our weekends away at the lake had become a monthly tradition, one the rest of the stallions were slightly jealous of. Not that they had a reason to be—each one got plenty of time with me. Special time where I made sure they each felt like a king and got to enjoy my undivided attention. We also had a lot of herd time together—sometimes naked, sometimes not.

I had somehow stumbled into a paradise of hot, sexy men who all loved me without reason. I was very, very blessed.

The sun beat down on my bikini-clad body, my belly warm and my soul happy. I loved my quiet time with Tripp. Loved the way he'd throw me around in the lake then settle in to read a book to me and the baby. Each stallion was convinced the child was his—Tripp, included—though we'd never know. We didn't need to. Our herd would grow, and the child would belong to all of us. One big, happy family.

An impatient one, apparently. The sound of hoofbeats moving closer broke the quiet peacefulness of our retreat, making Tripp sigh.

"Time to go home, doll."

"Or we could all stay right here." I sat up with Tripp's help, my hand falling immediately to my baby bump. I gave my men a big smile when they rounded the cabin and came racing up to where Tripp and I sat. "Good afternoon, boys. Y'all come to go skinny-dipping with me?"

Tripp laughed, reaching around to palm my belly. "You're such a little vixen."

"Guilty." Pregnancy had made me needier than usual—for sweets, for affection, and for sex. Quinn liked to joke that I was wearing them out, but deep down, I think they all loved it. I'd started dropping in on them in the middle of the night, picking a bed to crawl into and waking up that stallion with my mouth on their cock or by straddling their shoulders and rubbing my pussy over their lips and chin. No one complained. In fact, they seemed to enjoy not knowing when I'd come for them. In the barn, at the kitchen table, in their rooms...wherever and whenever. I'd drop to my knees or crawl onto their laps and say please. They always appreciated my politeness enough to make me come at least three times.

Seriously...paradise.

Tripp pinched my nipple and slid his hand over my pussy to caress my clit through the thin fabric covering it, bringing me back to the here and now. To the fact that my entire herd had shifted and were all stalking across the grass toward us. Looking so damn hot and ready for me.

"What's the game this time?" Tripp asked, leaning down to bite my neck as he teased me. "You want us all at once? A couple at a time? Or one-on-one?"

I couldn't help but stare at my herd as they stopped in front of me. All that beautiful skin. All those hard cocks. All *mine*. I rode Tripp's hand a little harder, circling my hips as the rest of the men watched. Knowing whatever happened next truly was up to me.

"One-on-one, I think..." I pursed my lips and pointed. "Eeny-meeny-miney-moe, caught my stallions by their toes, they can holler, but I'll never let go, eeny-meeny-miney-moe." I landed on Matthew, who'd healed nicely even if he had added a few scars to his physique. I hadn't been kidding the night Chance had hit him with the tractor—scars were hot. I liked licking his. "Your turn, Matthew."

Though, really, it was my turn. It was always my turn. And as the rest of the herd raced off to splash around in the cool lake water, Matthew picked me up and carried me inside the cabin. Looking like a man who'd won the lottery.

I understood that look.

I was pretty sure I wore it every day as well.

Seven men, seven stallions, one herd. All mine.

My herd. My heart. My lovers.

Mine forever.

Acknowledgments

There aren't enough words in the world to describe my respect for my editor, Lisa Hollett. Even when I do stupid things (like publish a book without letting her read it because I want to play in KU).

My readers make all the late nights, super early mornings, and excessive amounts of coffee worthwhile. Thank you for giving me the chance to tell my stories.

Y'all know I live for my daughters. No need to repeat myself.

Also By Ellis Leigh

Claiming His Chance

Claiming His Prize

———

THE GATHERING TALES

Come and enjoy tales from the biggest shifter event of the year as wolves from around the country fall in lust, in love, and in fate at The Gathering.

Killian and Lyra

Gideon and Kalie

Blasius, Dante, and Moira

Homecoming

Also available in one convenient anthology in both electronic and paperback formats.

The Gathering Tales

———

THE DEVIL'S DIRES

There's no escaping a Dire Wolf on the hunt...

Savage Surrender

Savage Sanctuary

Savage Seduction

Savage Silence

Savage Sacrifice

Savage Security

Savage Salvation (Coming Winter of 2018)

———

Have you met Kristin Harte?

Contemporary romantic suspense with heat.

Justice, Colorado

Where the vigilantes have all the legal authority.

In Justice, Colorado, the Kennards run everything, including the only big business in the area. Their sawmill employs most of the town, and the Kennard brothers live up to a long family history of keeping their neighbors and coworkers safe—until a motorcycle club comes to town and starts causing trouble. Big trouble.

The kind that ends in funerals.

The kind no law enforcement can help them with.

PAYBACK

RETALIATE

JUSTIFY

REPARATION

Sign up for Kristin Harte's newsletter so you never miss out on anything Justice related.

www.kristinharte.com/newsletter

About the Author

A storyteller from the time she could talk, Ellis grew up among family legends of hauntings, psychics, and love spanning decades. Those stories didn't always have the happiest of endings, so they inspired her to write about real life, real love, and the difficulties therein. From farmers to werewolves, store clerks to witches—if there's love to be found, she'll write about it. Ellis lives in the Chicago area with her two daughters and a German Shepherd that never leaves her side.

When she's not writing paranormal romance, Ellis Leigh can be found writing romantic suspense as Kristin Harte and erotic shorts as London Hale.

Sign up for Ellis Leigh's newsletter for release information, promotions, swag opportunities, and early access to free reads!

www.ellisleigh.com/newsletter.

For new release announcements only, follow Ellis on Bookbub.

Come join my reader group for fun, snippets, secret handshakes, and discussions of what I'm working on and when that next book will be out.

Ellis' Elite Reader Group

———

www.ingramcontent.com/pod-product-compliance
Lightning Source LLC
Chambersburg PA
CBHW050525190726
48284CB00003B/941